Emily Sneller

Elizabeth Gail and the Music Camp Romance

Hilda Stahl

Tyndale House Publishers, Inc., Wheaton, Illinois

Dedicated with love to the Duncans—
Jim, Ruth, Alex, Sonya, Rachel, Peter, Steve, & Donna

Cover and interior illustrations by Mort Rosenfeld

Library of Congress Catalog Card Number 88-51671
ISBN 0-8423-0808-3
Copyright 1983 by Hilda Stahl
Printed in the United States of America

95 94 93 92 91 90
10 9 8 7 6 5 4 3 2

Contents

ONE
A walk with Kyle

Elizabeth jerked a brush through her shoulder-length, curly brown hair as she nervously looked around the small cabin at her three roommates still asleep on their narrow cots. What would she say to them if they awoke and asked her where she was going so early in the morning? A fly buzzed at the small window and it seemed so loud she thought it might awaken the girls. And she wanted them to stay asleep until she was gone.

She gnawed her bottom lip and her hand trembled as she silently lay the brush on the dresser that she shared with Belinda.

Elizabeth looked toward the locked door. Would Kyle Grey really be waiting for her near the water fountain? Why had he asked her to go for a walk with him? There were other girls in the music camp who were dying to go with him—pretty girls who yearned for a wild romance with the handsome lifeguard. He knew she was a serious piano student, yet he'd asked her to spend time with him.

She shrugged. Maybe she was making too much of this walk. She wouldn't even consider going, but she wanted to convince herself that she wasn't losing her heart over Jerry Grosbeck. Sure, he was at home and she wouldn't see him for the rest of this month, but she didn't even want to think about him. She wasn't ready to have a steady boyfriend, and Jerry had insisted that they go only with each other.

She clamped her mouth tightly closed as she lifted her jacket off a wire hanger and slipped it on. She was going to be a famous concert pianist. She didn't have time to get serious over a boy, even one she loved as much as she loved Jerry Grosbeck.

Elizabeth reached for the lock on the door just as Aster sighed and turned over. Elizabeth froze, her eyes glued to Aster. Finally Elizabeth eased the lock open, then the door. Fresh, cool wind rushed in. Birds sang gaily in the surrounding pine trees. A squirrel scolded noisily.

Just outside the cabin Elizabeth sighed deeply as she rubbed her damp palms down her jeans. Her light jacket was enough to keep the cool wind out.

Would Kyle Grey show up or had he been teasing her?

She grinned and wrinkled her straight nose. What did it matter? It was great to be outdoors on such a beautiful morning with pine trees scenting the air. Now that she was over the little twinge of homesickness that she'd suffered last week, she could really enjoy music camp and the people she'd met. She grinned. Well, *most* of the people. Aster wasn't all that great. Jenny was all right, but she seemed to think she was Aster's shadow even outside the cabin. But Belinda was super. Most of the time it was fun to share a cabin with the three girls. As long as Aster forgot to be stuck up and jealous, that is.

Elizabeth laughed softly. She was tall and thin and

not at all beautiful. Aster had no reason to be jealous of her. And Aster had many, many friends, since this was her second year at Pine Valley Music Camp.

A fox squirrel scampered up a nearby pine, then sat on a limb, chattering noisily at Elizabeth as she walked on the pine needle-covered path. She tugged her blue corduroy jacket over her jeans. Her blue tennis shoes kept her steps quiet. Suddenly she wanted to leap high, twirl around, and shout at the top of her lungs.

If she was home right now, she'd do just that. On the Johnson farm no one would hear if she shouted for joy. A laugh bubbled up inside and burst out. Once she'd been a lonely, unloved, foster kid without a real home. But the Johnsons had adopted her. They loved her. They had loved her even when she was mean. She was Elizabeth Gail Johnson now, and she was sixteen years old and someday she'd be a famous concert pianist.

Susan, Ben, and Kevin had been born into the Johnson family. She and Toby had been adopted. The whole family had been glad that she had the chance to spend the month of July at Pine Valley Music Camp. Kevin had said he'd ride Snowball often and keep her brushed and fed. Susan had said she'd keep Jerry from being so lonely. Elizabeth frowned as she remembered that. Let Susan go with Jerry once in a while. So what? That's what she wanted, wasn't it?

"I will not think about Jerry Grosbeck!" whispered Elizabeth, doubling her fists.

She stopped at the fountain and watched the water drip around it. Maybe Kyle wouldn't come. She was too tall and too thin. How could a good-looking stranger be interested in her?

Jerry Grosbeck had said that he loved her, but that

9

was different. They'd both grown up as unloved, ragged aid kids, kicked from foster home to foster home. Then the Johnsons had prayed her into their family and loved her. Finally Jerry had found a family to love him, too. He was used to her looks, and he loved her anyway. Tears blurred her vision and for just a minute a great loneliness engulfed her.

Impatiently she rubbed away the tears. She was here to learn more about piano. Jerry was at home. He had said that he'd miss her, but he had said she had to go because of her career. Things like that made her love him more.

She frowned and shook her head. She would not continue this! She'd think about Kyle Grey. They would walk together and talk about music together. Kyle didn't have to know that once she'd had a mother who had beaten her and starved her and locked her in a closet. No one here at the music camp had to know anything about her past. To them she was Elizabeth Johnson. They didn't know that once she'd been Libby Dobbs, unloved and ugly.

She ran her finger around the fountain as she looked toward the long dining hall where she could hear someone whistling. She looked toward the deserted practice rooms and past them at other cabins. Where was Kyle?

A hand touched her shoulder and she whirled around with a startled gasp, her hazel eyes wide; then she laughed self-consciously. "Hi, Kyle."

He grinned and she liked the small dimple that appeared at the corner of his wide mouth. His dark blond hair looked as if he'd combed it quickly and his denim jacket collar was partially tucked in. "Hi, Elizabeth. I overslept. Sorry. Is it too late to walk awhile?"

She hesitated, then shook her head. He was at least as tall as Jerry, but fair, where Jerry was dark. "Where shall we go first?"

His dark blue eyes twinkled. "I saw something you might like to see when I ran through the woods just now."

She frowned slightly, her head tipped. "Were you in the woods already?"

He nodded. "Just to come meet you." He tugged at his collar, then turned it down properly.

"Where is your cabin?"

"Cabin? Oh! Hey, I just work here as a lifeguard at the pool. I'm not a student. I live about a mile from here."

She fell into step beside him as they left the path to follow an almost invisible trail. "I guess when you came to the practice room yesterday and talked to me about piano, I just assumed that you were a music student like the rest of us." She saw a strange look cross his face, then quickly disappear. Had she said something that bothered him?

"I like music, especially piano." He smiled down at her. "You play beautifully."

"Thank you. Do you play?"

He scowled and a pinched look appeared around his mouth. "No."

"You know so much about piano and about music. Haven't you ever wanted to make music yourself?"

"No!"

His answer was very sharp, and she snapped her mouth shut and stared down at the leaves and needles on the ground.

The silence between them pressed in on her and she

frantically searched for something to say. Nothing came to mind and she wanted to run back to the dining hall to wait for breakfast.

"Tell me about the farm you live on," said Kyle as if he hadn't just snapped at her minutes before.

She managed a smile. "It's a big farm with lots of animals. I have a white mare named Snowball. I love to ride. I remember when I first learned; it felt as though the horse was twenty feet high and I was afraid I'd fall off. But I didn't." She laughed up at him. "Do you ride? Since your home is in the country, I suppose it's a farm."

He shook his head. "Not a farm, just a house away from town. But I learned to ride at my uncle's. I like horses." He held a low branch aside for her, then let it flop back in place behind them. "Do you have brothers and sisters?"

She nodded. "One sister and three brothers. Do you?"

His face turned white and she was afraid he was going to faint or something. She touched his arm in panic, but he shrugged her hand off and turned away from her.

"I'm sorry, Kyle. Did I say something to upset you?"

He took a deep breath, then turned back and his coloring was normal again. "Sorry. I did have a sister."

Elizabeth bit her bottom lip to keep from asking about his sister. She could tell it was a painful subject to him and she didn't know him well enough to intrude on it.

He walked beside her without speaking again for a few minutes, then said, "From now on we'll have to be very quiet."

She stopped, her eyes wide. "Are you sure I'll want to see this?"

He grinned. "Sure you will. Just wait."

She sighed and walked on with him. He touched her

arm and she stopped abruptly, looking up questioningly.

"Stay close." His breath fanned her cheek and his hand closed over hers.

She looked at their clasped hands and felt a momentary quiver of fear.

He led her around a large poplar, then stopped her at a low-branched pine. Carefully he pulled a branch down and whispered in her ear, "Look."

She peeked through and her eyes grew big and round and her breath caught in her throat. Two bear cubs rolled around on the ground while their mother rooted at a trunk of a large oak.

Elizabeth clutched at Kyle's sleeve, her heart racing. Never in her life had she been this close to bears outside the zoo! Oh, but Kevin and Toby would like to see them!

The mother bear stood on her hind legs and looked nearsightedly toward Elizabeth and Kyle. Elizabeth's mouth went dry and she shrank back into Kyle. He wrapped his arm around her and held her close. Finally the bear dropped and turned to her cubs as they slapped playfully at each other.

Several minutes later Kyle whispered, "We have to go."

Reluctantly she walked with him away from the bears. Her eyes sparkled as she looked up at him.

"I didn't know bears lived wild around here. It's exciting, but scary!"

He stopped, his eyes narrowed. "You don't need to be afraid of bears, Beth."

Beth? No one had ever called her Beth. She'd been called Libby for years, and now Elizabeth. But if he wanted to call her Beth, so what? "I'm a little afraid, but not with you here. Are they very dangerous?"

He rubbed his hand across his forehead, then laughed

a tight little laugh. "If you leave them alone, they'll leave you alone. There's a dump near here and they feed from that. I see them often."

"Are you sure they won't harm us?"

He shook his head. "Only if you mess with the cubs or one is injured. I wouldn't let them hurt you, Elizabeth. I wouldn't let anything hurt you." He lifted her hand and rubbed it. "You are a pianist. Nothing must happen to you."

She swallowed hard. There was something about Kyle's manner that frightened her a little. "I think we'd better get back before we miss breakfast."

"Follow me." He took off, his long legs moving fast and she was forced to run to keep up with him. No way would she stay in the woods alone with bears so close!

On the path Kyle stopped and waited for her. Her face was flushed and damp with perspiration.

"See you later, Elizabeth. Enjoy your day."

She opened her mouth to speak but he dashed away. She stood with her hands on her narrow waist and shook her head. Something was wrong with Kyle Grey. But what could it be?

TWO
Trouble

Elizabeth stopped midstride, then turned and walked away from the dining hall. She could not walk in with Ned Everett and Mr. Brazer standing in the doorway talking. It was too early in the morning to see either of them, and to see them at the same time was really too much.

Just then Belinda called and waved and Elizabeth smiled in relief. Now she wouldn't have to go into breakfast alone.

"Where have you been, Elizabeth?" Belinda puffed to catch her breath. Her round face was red from hurrying. She was dressed in a plaid shirt and overalls. "I looked all over for you."

Elizabeth pushed her hands into her jacket pockets and hunched her slender shoulders. "I went for a walk with Kyle."

"Kyle Grey?"

"Yes."

"Oh! Oh, my!" Belinda clasped her hands together

over her heart. "That is the most romantic thing I've ever heard!"

Elizabeth laughed and shook her head. "We walked. He showed me some bears over there in the woods."

"Walking with Kyle Grey! Just wait until Aster hears about that! She'll be livid. Livid!" Belinda giggled.

"Let's go eat," said Elizabeth impatiently. The aromas of bacon and coffee were making her hungry.

"Aster and Jenny are already inside eating," said Belinda as they walked toward the hall. "I think I'll start a note around about your walk with Kyle just to see what Aster does."

Elizabeth caught her arm. "Don't you dare!"

"I was only teasing." Belinda's dark eyes twinkled mischievously. "You know me better than that."

"Sure I do." Elizabeth grinned and Belinda giggled. "Let's get in line before the food is gone." She glanced quickly to see that Ned and Mr. Brazer were in the line far enough ahead that she wouldn't have to speak to them. She flushed. She really shouldn't feel this way about them, but both of them in their own way made her feel uncomfortable.

"Who are you looking at that way?" asked Belinda in a low voice.

Elizabeth flushed. "I'll tell you later." She certainly didn't want to say anything about either Ned or Mr. Brazer and have them overhear. They both seemed to dislike her already without having more reason to.

With her plate filled with scrambled eggs, bacon, toast, and jelly, Elizabeth walked to an empty table far away from Ned, Mr. Brazer, and her two other roommates. She wanted to eat quietly, then go to practice without feeling upset over anything.

Belinda sat down, then leaned forward. "Aster and Jenny are looking at you. I wish I could tell them that you were with Kyle." She shook with silent laughter and Elizabeth frowned, her face red.

She poked her fork into her scrambled eggs, then looked up to meet Ned's eyes from across the room. Her stomach tightened and she quickly looked away. Why didn't he like her? He barely knew her, yet he was hostile toward her for some reason. Maybe she should walk right up to him and demand to know what his problem was. She couldn't stand to be on her guard against him the rest of the month.

The voices and clatter of silverware against plates almost blotted out the sounds of background music. Elizabeth ate slowly, talking with Belinda from time to time.

"I have to run back to the cabin for my flute," said Belinda as she dabbed her mouth with a white paper napkin. "I sure wish Mr. Brazer was my teacher instead of Ms. Kooms. He's such a lamb."

Elizabeth choked on a drink of water. She coughed and held her napkin to her mouth. Finally she said, "Mr. Brazer is awful! He yells at me if I make even a tiny mistake. He doesn't think I'll ever be a concert pianist."

Belinda shook her head. "But, Elizabeth, everyone loves Mr. Brazer. Well, everyone that I know.

"Why doesn't he like me? Why is he so hard on me?"

"I don't know." Belinda shrugged her plump shoulder. "Maybe he's tired by the time you have him, so he takes it out on you."

Elizabeth pushed back her chair, then waited for Belinda. Elizabeth pulled her jacket off the back of her chair and slipped it on. She would never make Belinda

understand the hostility she felt coming from Mr.
Brazer. She couldn't understand it herself.

Outside as they walked toward the fountain Belinda
gripped Elizabeth's arm. "There he is!" she whispered,
shaking Elizabeth's arm. "Oh! I wish I was tall and
slender and gorgeous like you."

Elizabeth blinked. Gorgeous? She was far from
gorgeous. She followed Belinda's gaze, but couldn't tell
who had made her so excited.

"Isn't he the best-looking boy you've ever seen? Right
next to Kyle Grey, if you ask me!" Belinda locked her
hands together as she stared across the yard.

"Who are you talking about, Belinda?"

"You know! Barney Little! He's so tall and
absolutely beautiful!"

Elizabeth laughed, then bit her tongue. Belinda had
every right to think Barney was "absolutely beautiful,"
even if he wasn't. "You'd better hurry back to the cabin
and get your flute."

"Now? In the presence of that?"

"Come on, silly." Elizabeth tugged Belinda along with
her to the cabin. "You'll have to admire Barney during
your free time. You should be thinking of the piece
you're going to play for the audition."

"I already know what I'm going to play. And I'm going
to be chosen to play with the symphony!" Belinda
nodded with determination, then wrinkled her small
nose. "Besides, Barney's going to audition, too."

Elizabeth laughed and shook her head. "I give up,
Belinda. You're going to think about boys no matter
what I say."

"Look who's talking! The girl who walked with Kyle

Grey this morning. Somehow, I don't think your only interest in life is concert piano."

Elizabeth stopped, her jaw set. "But it is! I have a dream and nothing will stop me from fulfilling it!"

"Hey!" Belinda touched Elizabeth's arm. "Relax, will you? You can be a great concert pianist and still have normal feelings toward boys."

"Right now I'm only interested in getting my music so I can get back to the practice room before I get a demerit." She opened the cabin door and walked in, then stopped dead. An envelope lay on the floor at the foot of her cot. She picked it up, her hand trembling. Just as she thought! She held it up. "All right, Belinda! Who's been reading my letter from Susan?"

Belinda flushed and backed against the door. "Not me! Really! It was Aster. I told her not to read it, but she just laughed and said she would if she wanted to."

Elizabeth gripped the letter and sank to the edge of her cot. Susan had written, pleading with her to spend more time with Jerry and to go with him only. And Aster had dared to read it!

The door opened and Elizabeth jumped up, her hazel eyes flashing. The letter crackled in her hand. "How dare you, Aster!"

Aster tossed back her dark hair. "What's the big deal about the letter? I happen to think you should hang onto Jerry and ignore the boys around here." She laughed.

"It's not funny! My life is none of your business!" Elizabeth's chest rose and fell in agitation. She wanted to do something violent, but she forced herself to stand still. She saw Jenny's white face and Belinda's concern.

19

"I'm willing to forget this, Aster, but stay away from my things from now on."

Aster smiled a wicked little smile, then bent to pick up her violin and music.

"She won't do it again," said Jenny in a low, tight voice, her hands clenched on her pile of music.

"I don't need you to talk for me, Jenny," snapped Aster.

Elizabeth stuffed the letter in her purse, picked up her music, and rushed out of the cabin with Belinda close behind. Elizabeth was so angry she could hear the blood pounding in her ears. Why did Aster want to make trouble?

"Are you all right?" asked Belinda.

Elizabeth nodded. How could she concentrate on her playing now? Was it really worth staying at Pine Valley? Maybe she should call home and tell them she wanted to go home. Chuck would pick her up at the bus station.

"What are you thinking, Elizabeth?" Belinda was running to keep up with Elizabeth's long, angry strides.

Suddenly Elizabeth stopped, her music books clutched to her. "I might as well go home. How can I play when I'm upset?"

"You can! You are a professional! Don't let Aster ruin it for you!" Tears filled Belinda's dark eyes.

Elizabeth walked on, her head high. It wasn't just Aster. It was Ned and Mr. Brazer.

"Think of your career, Elizabeth. Nothing should stand in your way. Don't let anyone take that away from you!"

She was right and Elizabeth knew it. She stopped again and smiled down at Belinda. "You're right. Thanks."

"Sure. What're friends for?"

Elizabeth smiled. "I'll see you at lunch, Belinda. And thanks again."

"Anytime."

Elizabeth ran to the practice room and closed the door just as the eight o'clock bell rang. Quickly she dropped her jacket on the hook near the door, then sat at the upright piano and opened the first book. She played "Spinning Song" by Albert Elmenreich and the music soothed her.

As she reached for another book, she heard a fly buzz at the window. She glanced at it, then froze. Kyle stood just outside the window, watching her intently. His eyes met hers and he flushed, then disappeared from sight. She shivered, then laughed at herself. So what if he had watched and listened to her?

But why hadn't he stepped inside to talk to her as he had yesterday? He didn't have to spy on her.

She frowned impatiently. "Spy?" She rolled her eyes. She'd spent too much time around Kevin, who was planning on being a detective when he grew up.

She touched the piano keys. Kyle wouldn't bother her. He just liked piano music. Didn't he?

THREE
Mr. Brazer

Elizabeth gathered up her music, then turned at the
sound of the door opening. Maybe Kyle had decided to
talk with her after all. But it was Ned Everett and he
was frowning. Her stomach tightened.

"Your time was up five minutes ago," he said sharply.
As he stopped beside her she noticed that he was
shorter than she. He looked younger than seventeen
years old. "This is my practice hour now."

"Sorry." She walked toward the door, then turned
back, her brows lifted questioningly. "Ned, have I done
something to upset you? We barely know each other,
but for some reason you either snap at me or glare at
me every time we meet. What's wrong?" Her mouth felt
dry as she waited for his answer. Maybe she didn't want
to know why he didn't like her. Maybe she should walk
out before he told her what he thought of her.

Ned dropped his pile of music on the bench, then
looked at Elizabeth, his brown eyes thoughtful. He
looked more like a gymnast than a future concert
pianist. "I don't know what you're talking about. I'm

here to further my career. I don't have time to waste thinking up an answer for your strange questions."

She flushed. At times she knew that her insecurity showed, but she really had thought he disliked her. "Sorry."

He shrugged slightly. He rested his hands on his hips and waited.

"I have a few minutes before I have to be in class with Mr. Brazer. Could I listen to you play?"

He frowned. "Why should you want to?"

"I love piano and I've heard that you're very good." She moved restlessly from one foot to the other.

He narrowed his dark eyes. "You want to evaluate the competition."

"What?" She would not get angry! She clutched her books tighter as he stepped toward her.

"You and I are competing for the piano lead in the symphony."

She shook her head. "No. There are several piano students here."

"But we're the best! And only one can be chosen. The auditions are next week."

She hugged her music books tighter. She wanted to play for the symphony. Rachael Avery had told her about this in her last piano lesson before she'd come to Pine Valley. "I know you want the part."

"And I know you do, too."

Elizabeth nodded. She hadn't given a thought to the ones who wouldn't be chosen, but now she knew how disappointing it would be for Ned. As much as it would for her. "We both can't be chosen."

"No." He rubbed his brown hair back from his narrow face. "No, we can't. I'm determined to get it and that's why you're getting out of here right now. I must practice."

She turned and fumbled with the knob and finally opened the door and stepped out into the bright morning sunlight. Sounds of music came from other practice rooms. Others were determined to be chosen for the symphony. But they had more of a chance because there were several instruments in each section of the orchestra, whereas only one piano was needed for this concert. She sighed and her shoulders drooped. She was good, but was she good enough to beat Ned?

What would she do if she wasn't chosen?

She shivered. How could she endure sitting in the audience instead of at the piano performing?

She glanced at her watch, then gasped. She had one minute to get to her lesson. With Mr. Brazer as teacher, she didn't want to be late.

A minute later she rushed into the classroom and Mr. Brazer turned from the piano and glared at her.

"You're five minutes late, Miss Johnson."

She bit her lip. "My watch says I'm right on time."

"Then fix your watch!" He was short and stocky with thinning gray hair and gray eyes that looked steely as Elizabeth rushed to set her music on the baby grand. One book tumbled to the floor and her face burned. She had never been this nervous with Rachael Avery. If only Rachael were here and her teacher! Mr. Brazer was just too stern.

Elizabeth sat on the bench and opened the book that he told her to. Her fingers felt stiff and she flexed them self-consciously. Didn't Mr. Brazer know that he was making her nervous? Or didn't he care?

Her stomach tightened as she played. She stumbled

over a note, then continued on. This time her music didn't soothe her. Mr. Brazer's soft breathing over her shoulder irritated her and she wanted to tell him to step back.

"Play it again, Elizabeth," he said, clicking his tongue. "A second-year student could do better than that. Watch your timing. Read the notes and give me a feel of the piece."

She nodded, then played it again. She knew she was doing badly and her anger rose.

"Miss Johnson, I know you see yourself as a concert pianist, but you are deluding yourself."

She gasped and turned to stare at him. How could he say that to her? Rachael had often said that she would be a concert pianist and Rachael would know. For years Rachael Avery had traveled around giving concerts. She'd been one of the best until she'd given up her career to raise a family. How could Mr. Brazer stand there and say such a terrible thing?

"Don't look so stricken, Elizabeth." He tapped his yellow pencil in the palm of his hand. "We can't all be winners. We can't all see our dreams become realities."

She lifted her pointed chin and her hazel eyes flashed. "Mr. Brazer, I will be a concert pianist! I will!"

He shook his head. "Not possible."

She spun around and leaped to her feet. "It is possible! I can play! I don't know why you're doing this to me."

"Sit down! Sit down and put that fire into your playing instead of blazing at me!" He pointed to the bench and finally she sank back down. He thumped the book and she struck the chord, then played. She would show him what she could do!

When she finished she looked up in triumph. She knew she'd played exceptionally well.

"Better," he said gruffly. "But not good enough. You must learn to play no matter what the circumstances around you are, no matter what your personal feelings are. You must put yourself totally into your music. I don't believe you can do it. I think that you've been coddled for too long."

The words buzzed inside her head. Blood pounded in her ears and she doubled her fists in rage. A few years ago she would have screamed and cursed, but she kept the words back. It had taken a long time, but with God's help she'd learned to control her temper. At least most of the time. She bit her bottom lip and her chest rose and fell as he explained what he wanted her to practice.

Finally he excused her and she walked stiffly from the room, her books pressed to her racing heart. Oh, she never, never wanted to see him again!

Outdoors, she ran away from the other students so that she wouldn't have to talk. If she opened her mouth, she knew she'd burst into tears.

She reached her cabin and stepped inside and locked the door. Giant tears filled her eyes, then slowly ran down her flushed cheeks.

"Oh, that man! That terrible, terrible man!"

She dropped down on her cot and wrapped her arms around her almost boy-thin body and rocked back and forth. "Heavenly Father, I need your help and your comfort right now. I don't like Mr. Brazer. I'm so angry at him!"

She stopped, her eyes wide. God wanted her to forgive Mr. Brazer and to love him. She sniffed and rubbed her fist across her nose.

"I'm sorry, Father. You'll have to help me forgive Mr. Brazer. I know that you gave me a dream to be a concert pianist. I know that you are helping me to become one. You will have to love that man through me because on my own, I can't love him."

Elizabeth prayed for several minutes, then wiped away her tears. She wasn't alone in this. She had a heavenly Father who cared. She reached for her Bible and read, then smiled. God was her strength and her help. He was her comfort. He was always with her, no matter what the circumstances. She would not let Mr. Brazer's words harm her. She would be a concert pianist! Nothing and no one would stop her!

She closed her eyes and pictured herself walking out on the stage of a great auditorium. She could see the audience as they applauded. She could see herself playing, playing with her entire being until the audience was totally captivated.

She laughed aloud and her fingers tingled at the thought of giving her music to others in such a beautiful way.

"I will make it!" she whispered fiercely. "I will!"

She remembered the audition and slumped, her fingers twined together nervously. If Ned played better, then he would be the solo pianist.

A cricket chirped in the corner of the cabin and birds sang outdoors. Elizabeth jumped up, her eyes wide. She must practice again. She must spend every minute practicing.

If Kyle asked her to go walking with him again, she'd turn him down. She nodded, then shrugged with a grin. Why even think about that? Kyle wouldn't bother with her, not when Aster was around and willing.

Elizabeth gathered up her books and walked to the door. Kyle stood there, his hand lifted to knock.

"Hi," he said, grinning. "It's lunch time and I couldn't find you at the dining hall."

"Were you looking for me?" Her heart skipped a beat and she frowned impatiently.

"I thought we could eat together and talk. I don't want to take up your practice time later."

She smiled. How could she argue with that? She fell into step beside him. The shade from the pines kept the hot sun off her. "Kyle, what do you know about Mr. Brazer?"

Kyle stiffened. "I've heard he's an excellent teacher, but strict. Why?"

"He's rough on me." She could've bitten her tongue off for saying that to Kyle. "I don't mean that he isn't a good teacher, you understand. He just doesn't seem to like me."

Kyle stopped abruptly and caught Elizabeth's free hand. "Don't you worry about that man! You are going to be the best pianist around. When he sees you play in front of thousands of people, then he'll be sorry he yelled at you. He'll be sorry he didn't give you the lead in the symphony."

Her heart seemed to stop, then crashed on. "What do you mean, Kyle?"

"Beth, you can't let that man get you down!"

Elizabeth stepped back. A shiver ran down her spine. "Kyle?"

He blinked, then cleared his throat.

"Oh, Elizabeth. Did I call you Beth again?" He laughed and it sounded strained to Elizabeth.

"Who's Beth, Kyle?"

He pushed his long fingers through his dark blond hair. "My sister. She plays the piano, too."

"Is she here?"

Kyle shook his head. "Last year. She was here last year." A sad look darkened his blue eyes. "She played the piano."

"I'd like to hear her sometime. Is she good?"

Kyle stuffed his hands into his jeans pockets and hunched his broad shoulders. "Beth is the best."

Elizabeth saw the strained look on his face. "I take it Mr. Brazer gave her a hard time, too."

"Yes! I wanted to punch him, but Beth wouldn't let me. She wouldn't let me!" Kyle tipped back his head and closed his eyes in a scowl. "I wish I had! I wish I had knocked him down for Beth!"

Elizabeth awkwardly touched Kyle's arm. "Are you all right?"

Kyle kicked a pinecone and sent it skittering among the trees. "We'd better get to lunch before it's too late."

"All right," she said uncertainly. What caused his strange change of moods? She fell into step beside him. Maybe she should excuse herself and go to lunch alone, or even go right to the practice room. She hesitated, then barely shook her head. It was only lunch. What could it hurt?

FOUR
New development

Elizabeth wearily pushed herself to the edge of the swimming pool. Water streamed down her head and shoulders and off her blue flowered swimsuit. She wiped her eyes with her hands. The hot sun felt good against her bare back. She squeezed the ends of her hair, then pushed it back off her face.

Behind her she could hear Aster talking with Kyle. Splashing and laughing blocked out parts of the conversation, but Elizabeth could hear enough to know that Aster was asking Kyle to drive into town with her to see a movie. Elizabeth held her breath and waited for his answer. It really didn't matter. It didn't! Kyle didn't have to go to the practice room with her to listen to her and to talk about music with her as he had the past three evenings. She could practice alone. She frowned. Was she becoming too dependent on Kyle? Was he becoming too important to her? She frowned and strained her ears to hear Kyle.

"No, Aster," Kyle said sharply. "I told you I can't. I have plans."

Elizabeth smiled a pleased little smile. Of course he meant he had plans with her. Oh, but she'd love to turn around and look at Aster.

"Kyle, we had so much fun last year. I know we could this year if you'd let us," said Aster.

"Last year was different," said Kyle sharply.

"Because of Beth?" asked Aster and Elizabeth waited tensely.

"I'm here to work, Aster, not carry on a conversation," said Kyle gruffly and Elizabeth frowned thoughtfully. She'd have to learn what had happened to Beth and upset Kyle so much. Each time she'd tried to ask him about his sister, he'd clammed right up.

From the corner of her eye Elizabeth saw Aster step to the edge of the pool, then shout for Jenny.

"I'm ready to go, Jenny. Can't you come right now when I want you to?"

Jenny pushed herself out of the pool and grabbed her towel to follow Aster. Elizabeth wanted to catch Jenny and tell her that Abraham Lincoln had freed the slaves years ago. Elizabeth sighed. Jenny needed a real friend, not one like Aster.

Later Elizabeth slipped on her beach jacket and grabbed her towel. "Bye, Kyle," she called. Her cheeks grew warm as she realized that she'd called to him just to give him a chance to tell her that he'd see her later.

He lifted his hand and smiled, but didn't say anything and she turned away, disappointed, and walked slowly toward her cabin. Just because he hadn't agreed to go with Aster to the movie didn't mean that he was going to be with her in the practice room. She was a big girl now and she didn't need someone with her all the time to cheer her on or even to keep her from being lonely.

She swatted a thirsty mosquito off her long bare leg and wriggled her toes in her sandals. Why was she allowing her mind to dwell so much on Kyle Grey?

She swung her damp towel around her neck and pushed the disturbing question away. She should be thinking about Tchaikovsky's Piano Concerto No. 1. Mr. Brazer said that she needed to get the mood right as well as the notes. Kyle had helped her.

She frowned. Kyle again?

Was he going to join her in the practice room again tonight?

She stopped at the fountain and looked toward the practice rooms. The sounds of a violin and an oboe drifted from the rooms. The sun disappeared behind a hill. In the shade of the pines the air was cooler and Elizabeth shivered. She had to get off her wet suit and slip on dry clothes. If she had time she'd write a quick letter home before practicing again.

She pushed open the cabin door, then stopped as Aster and Jenny looked up as if they'd been caught in the middle of something that they weren't supposed to be doing.

"Hi, girls." Elizabeth managed a smile as she dropped her towel over a rack to dry.

"We have to leave, Elizabeth," said Jenny quickly, awkwardly picking up her music and her oboe.

"We have time," said Aster as she pushed something into her dresser drawer.

Elizabeth found dry clothes and dropped them on the cot.

Jenny cleared her throat. "Remember that we have to meet Rachel Duncan in just a few minutes so we can practice together."

Aster frowned and pulled on a sweater. "All right, Jenny."

Elizabeth watched them walk to the door. Aster turned her head and smiled as if she knew a secret and Elizabeth frowned. What was Aster up to now?

The minute the door closed behind them, Elizabeth reached into her pillowcase for Jerry's letter. She sighed in relief. The letter was still there. It would be terrible if Aster read Jerry's letter!

Elizabeth pushed the letter back into the pillowcase, then hurried to the showers. The warm water felt good against her cool skin. The shampoo soon took all the smell of chlorine out of her hair.

Several minutes later she walked back into the cabin, feeling clean and refreshed. The jeans and dark pink sweater felt comfortably warm.

A cricket chirped in a far corner and Elizabeth jumped, then laughed softly. She should be enjoying this quiet time instead of feeling nervous about being alone.

She pulled out Jerry's letter and carefully unfolded it. Her stomach tightened. Aster must never read this letter.

"Oh, Jerry, Jerry," Elizabeth whispered. She rubbed the letter gently and her eyes misted over with sad tears. He wanted so much more of her time and feelings than she could give right now.

She sighed as she looked once again at the letter.

Dear Elizabeth,

I miss you so much. It seems like you've been gone a month already, but I know it hasn't been that long. But I am glad that you had this wonderful opportunity. Your dream is coming true. That little aid kid that nobody wanted is going to be famous someday. And I'll walk

*around with my chest puffed out with pride and tell them
you're my girl.*

*My summer job gets a little boring. But maybe it's
because you're not here to talk to. Susan and I
sometimes do things together. She's trying to cheer me
up, but nothing can make me really happy these days.
Except you, Elizabeth.*

*Ben and I are helping your dad hay. Ben loves it, but I'd
rather work at something else. I wore a short-sleeved shirt
the first day and that was a big mistake. My arms were so
scratched that I didn't think they'd ever heal. Your mom
rubbed aloe vera gel on me and the next day it was hard to
tell I'd been scratched. I've been wearing a long-sleeved
shirt now.*

*Elizabeth, I love you so much! I wish you were here
right now so I could hold you close and kiss you. We belong
together, Elizabeth. You're the only girl for me. I love you!*

Tears stung her eyes and Elizabeth quickly folded
the letter and slipped it back into the envelope and
into her pillowcase.

How could Jerry say that she was the only girl for
him? How could he know that?

"Oh, Jerry," she whispered. She dabbed the tears
away and pulled out a piece of stationery and a
matching envelope. She rubbed her finger across the
girl holding a bouquet of daisies at the corner of the paper.

She sat at the desk in the corner and wrote to Jerry,
telling him about the music she'd been working on,
about swimming, about seeing the bears, but she didn't
say anything about Kyle. She looked down at her
slanted writing with a frown. Why didn't she just tell
Jerry that she'd met Kyle and at first she'd thought he

was strange, then had grown to like him and enjoy having him around.

She sighed and shook her head. Jerry would be hurt if she mentioned Kyle. Jerry would think that she was falling in love with Kyle, and she wasn't. Not at all.

Was she?

She flushed and quickly finished the letter and stuffed it into the envelope. She licked a stamp and stuck it in place. Tomorrow she'd drop the letter in the box in the office when she picked up her mail, if she had any.

Belinda's alarm clock ticked loudly and Elizabeth glanced to see that it was almost eight. She stuffed the letter to Jerry in her purse, gathered up her music, and rushed out. She would not feel bad if Kyle wasn't waiting at the fountain for her. She wouldn't even wonder if he'd had a date with one of the girls who flocked around him at the pool.

A band tightened around her heart and she clutched her music books more tightly. The tall lights flashed on around the music camp and lit it up with a yellow tone. A whippoorwill called in the distance. A dog barked.

Elizabeth hesitated at the fountain. Kyle wasn't in sight and she almost burst into tears. She blinked fast and swallowed hard. She really could get along without Kyle Grey. She could!

Slowly she walked toward the practice rooms where light shone from each window and music drifted out and blended together to sound like an orchestra tuning up before a performance. Insects and peepers and deep-throated bullfrogs added to the grand performance.

Elizabeth stopped outside her practice room. She

36

could hear Ned playing Mozart's Piano Sonata in C and a thrill ran over her. She wanted to creep inside and sit and listen and absorb the music but she stood at the closed door. Ned would really be angry at her if she walked in to listen. My, but he could play!

Would he be chosen to perform instead of her?

She gripped her books more tightly. He was good, but so was she. Her heart beat faster and faster. Oh, she must not lose!

"Hello, Elizabeth."

She gasped in surprise, then laughed softly up at Kyle. "Hi."

"I didn't mean to startle you." He frowned toward the closed door. "Ned's time is up. He shouldn't take your time."

"He'll stop in a minute."

Kyle pushed open the door and light streamed out. "Your time is up, Ned."

Elizabeth tugged at Kyle's arm, but he brushed her aside and strode to the piano and clamped his hand on Ned's arm.

"Your time is up!"

Ned stopped midnote and scowled. "I was almost finished."

"You're finished right now." Kyle frowned down at Ned and Elizabeth shook her head.

"It's all right, Ned. Go ahead and finish. We don't mind listening. Do we, Kyle?" She frowned up at him, but he shook his head and said that Ned shouldn't take up her valuable practice time.

Ned gathered up his books, his face red, and slammed out.

Elizabeth stood with her hands on her waist. "Kyle, you didn't have to do that. He was leaving."

Kyle shrugged, then pulled off his lightweight jacket and dropped it over the back of a straight-backed chair. "He's gone, so forget it. Sit down and practice. I have been waiting for this special time together."

Her stomach fluttered strangely and she sat down on the bench and opened her first book. She smiled almost shyly at Kyle. Had he really been looking forward to being with her?

"Play, Beth." He flushed. "I mean . . . Elizabeth."

An hour later he walked her back to her cabin, her books in one of his large, strong hands. She stopped at the door and smiled up at him.

"I'll see you tomorrow, Kyle. Thanks for being with me. You're a lot of help."

He cupped her face in his free hand and her heart stood still, then leaped. "I enjoy just being with you, Elizabeth. Good night."

She waited, then flushed as she suddenly realized that she wanted him to kiss her good night. She fumbled with the knob, then finally turned it. "Good night, Kyle."

"Good night."

She stepped into the brightly lit cabin, then closed the door. Did her face give anything away? She saw Belinda giggle silently and Jenny quickly ducked her head. Aster laughed aloud.

"What is Jerry going to say when he finds out about Kyle Grey?" asked Aster, rubbing her hand on her robe sleeve.

Elizabeth clamped her mouth closed and dropped her

music on the foot of her cot. She wouldn't answer Aster. She wouldn't think about what she'd said.

"I went out with Kyle a lot last year," continued Aster, holding up her pink fingernails for minute inspection. "We had fun together. I knew his sister Beth. She played piano." Aster looked right at Elizabeth. "Just like you do."

"I know," said Elizabeth with a nonchalant shrug. She wanted to ask about Beth, but she bit her tongue to keep back the words.

"Beth is dead, you know."

Elizabeth stared at Aster and Belinda gasped in surprise.

Aster looked around the small cabin, then casually picked up her fingernail polish and screwed the lid back on.

"How did she die?" asked Belinda from where she sat on her cot.

Aster shrugged. "She was ice-skating and fell through the ice. Kyle hasn't been the same since."

Elizabeth dropped to the edge of her cot and wrapped her long arms around herself. Oh, poor Kyle!

A tear splashed on Elizabeth's arm, then another. She let them fall.

FIVE
Mixed-up love

Belinda pulled a brush through her auburn hair as she turned to Elizabeth. "I really think I'll be chosen to be in the symphony! Ms. Kooms said that I might be first-chair flute! Oh, I hope I get it!"

Elizabeth smiled. "I hope you do, too, Belinda. You're very good and you spend a lot of time practicing." Elizabeth slipped on her tan sandals and stood up. "And we'd both better get at it again."

"I'm too full from lunch, but I guess I could manage to practice if I walked around awhile first." Belinda buckled her overalls, then tugged them in place. "Maybe we'll run into Barney."

"Maybe." Elizabeth giggled.

"We had a beautiful talk last night." Belinda sighed and hugged her music to herself. "He thinks I play very well!"

Elizabeth held the cabin door open for Belinda. "You do play well, Belinda."

"I mean *very* well!" She nudged a pinecone with the

toe of her sandal. "I mean well enough to play in the symphony."

Elizabeth half listened as they walked down the shaded path. It was two days before her audition for the symphony. Her stomach tightened. The audition would be worse than any recital she'd ever played at. Mr. Brazer and Mr. Clearmont would be listening intently and judging harshly.

Belinda nudged Elizabeth. "There he is! You don't mind if I leave you, do you, Elizabeth?"

"You go ahead and walk with Barney. I'm sure I can make it on my own." Elizabeth laughed and wrinkled her nose. "You'd better call him and run to catch up to him."

Belinda flushed, then tossed her auburn hair back flippantly. "If that was Kyle instead of Barney, you'd be the one running off."

Elizabeth opened her eyes wide in mock surprise. "Me? What makes you think that?"

"I wonder." Belinda laughed, then hurried toward Barney, calling for him. He turned and waited for her, seeming very pleased to see her.

Elizabeth smiled and walked on alone. Where was Kyle right now? Maybe she could find him just to say hello before practice time. Maybe she could tell him that she knew about Beth and that she was sorry.

Tears stung her eyes. She stopped near the showers beside the pool. Splashing and laughing and shouting filled the air. This really wouldn't be a good time to mention Beth to Kyle. Elizabeth chewed her lip thoughtfully. She'd tried to tell Kyle several times in the past two days, but each time the opportunity had slipped by before she could find the courage and the right words.

She squared her shoulders and shifted her books higher in her arms, then walked around to where she knew Kyle would be on duty as lifeguard.

Her heart leaped as she saw him standing near his post. His long, lean body was tanned a copper tone and his blue trunks hugged his body and a whistle hung around his neck on a chain.

As Elizabeth stood admiring him, Aster walked up to him, looking her most provocative in a red bikini. Her body glistened with water from the pool and her long dark hair shone wetly. A pang of jealousy shot through Elizabeth and she started to turn away; then she stood still and watched them together. She was too far away to hear what they were saying, but she could tell that Kyle was angry and Aster was laughing.

Just then Kyle looked her way and she froze. Did he think she was spying on him? Maybe she should just walk up to him and say hello, then go to practice. She took a step forward, then stopped. The look on Kyle's face surprised and upset her. He was glaring at her. At *her*! He had been angry at Aster; now he was angry at her and her throat constricted painfully. She glanced at Aster and Aster was laughing, laughing at her!

Abruptly Elizabeth turned, almost bumping into Rachel Duncan, then rushed away from the pool. Her face burned with embarrassment and anger and a few emotions she couldn't identify, or didn't want to.

She stopped in the shade of a tall pine and took a deep breath. She shuddered, then closed her eyes and forced herself to calm down.

Maybe she'd read the entire scene wrong. What if

Kyle had been silently signaling for her to rescue him from Aster? Elizabeth groaned. It was too late to go back now. She had to get to practice.

A pine bough brushed against her head, and she pulled the needles from her curls as she walked toward the practice room. Lunch aromas still hung in the air along with the scent of pine.

"Heavenly Father," she whispered softly as she walked. "Take away these mixed-up feelings and help me to have a good practice time now."

She lifted her eyes toward heaven and smiled and whispered, "Thank you. I love you and I'm glad you love me and care about me."

She opened the door to the empty practice room. Someone's perfume still lingered in the air. She pushed open the window to let in a little breeze, then walked to the piano.

A plain white envelope with "Elizabeth Johnson" printed on it stood on the music stand. She dropped her books to the bench, then slowly reached for the envelope, her heart racing in alarm. Why would anyone leave a note like this for her?

The envelope crackled in her fingers as she gripped it more tightly. Slowly she turned it over and tore open the flap that was lightly sealed. Her hand shook as she pulled out the folded page inside.

She unfolded the page and looked down at the large hand-printed words. She read the words aloud in whispered anguish. "Someone knows that you are an aid kid. That person is going to make trouble for you. Be very careful!"

She sagged against the piano and her throat closed

painfully. Who had left the note for her? Who knew that she'd been an aid kid?

Awkwardly she pushed her music books over and sank down on the bench, her legs trembling. Noises from outdoors drifted through the open window. A fly buzzed between the window shade and windowpane.

Who knew that she'd been an aid kid?

Who wanted to make trouble for her?

She pressed her hand to her aching head and moaned. Ned wanted badly to play solo piano in the symphony. Would he make trouble for her so that he could get it?

Aster wanted Kyle for herself. Was she doing this?

Elizabeth shook her head, the note pressed to her heart, her eyes closed. This note would not stop her from doing what she wanted to do! It wouldn't stop her from being who she wanted to be! Oh, but she didn't want anyone to know that once she'd been an unloved, ugly aid kid without a real home. But if anyone did know it, what would it matter? Except for the blow to her pride, that is.

She flushed and looked down at the letter again. Had a friend or an enemy written it? Had Belinda heard something, but was afraid to speak to her face to face? No. Belinda wouldn't be afraid to do that—not Belinda.

Elizabeth rubbed her arm, then glanced at her watch. "Oh, dear! I must practice!" But how could she now? Her stomach was tied into a tight knot and her hands were trembling.

She stood a book in place and opened it to Bach's Invention No. 14. The page of black notes blurred before her eyes and she blinked hard. She had to practice no matter how she felt. She had to!

"You're a professional, Elizabeth Gail Johnson!" she said through clenched teeth. "You can play no matter what the circumstances!"

She squirmed on the bench, pushed her fingers through her curls, then started to play. Soon the music soothed her and surrounded her and engulfed her. The music was she and she was the music.

Finally she stopped. Wearily she bent her long neck and closed her eyes. A hand rested on her shoulder and she jumped. She turned her head to find Ned standing there, for once a smile on his face.

"I have never heard you play so well, Elizabeth."

She blinked in surprise. "Why, thank you, Ned!"

He stepped back and pulled his face into a frown. "Your time is up, you know."

"Oh, sorry. I didn't know. I wasn't thinking of time."

His brown eyes softened. "I could tell."

She gathered up her books, then spotted the open note on the floor near the bench. She dove for it and crumpled it before Ned could see it. But maybe he'd already seen it and read it. Or even written it. She narrowed her hazel eyes thoughtfully. "How come you're suddenly so nice to me?"

He flushed and stroked his cheek with one long finger with a blunt, square-cut nail. "Your music carried me away, I guess."

She eyed him suspiciously. "Oh?"

"It didn't hurt me to tell you that you play well. We both know it. We both know that I play just as well." He walked to the door and opened it for her. "Your time is up."

She held her books to her. She felt very tall and

awkward standing beside him. "I'd really like to stay to listen to you."

"Sure you would." He motioned her out and finally she sailed out the door, her back straight, her pointed chin high.

She looked around frantically. She didn't want anyone to know that she'd been tossed out again by Ned Everett.

Her jeans felt hot against her long legs as she ran head down into the shade of the pines along the path to her cabin. Suddenly she ran into someone and her books flew from her arms. She would have fallen but strong hands gripped her arms. She lifted her eyes.

"Oh, Kyle," she cried and immediately burst into tears.

"Did I hurt you?" he asked stiffly.

She sniffed and tried to stop crying, but sobs shook her thin body. "Ned just threw me out again." It was much more than that, but she couldn't say any more. She watched as he gathered up her books, then she saw the note and leaped for it with a strangled cry. Frantically she balled it into her hand.

"Is that a note from your boyfriend?"

"What?" she looked up into Kyle's angry face.

"Jerry Grosbeck. Remember him? He loves you and you love him."

"Oh." How had he found out? "He really isn't my boyfriend, Kyle." Her voice came out in a weak squeak.

"Do you love him?"

She hesitated, then nodded. "It's hard to explain, Kyle. I do love him, but we're going with others. We're not committed to each other."

"I see," he said coldly as he held the books out for her.

She took them and her hand brushed his and he

jerked back as if she'd burned him. "I can't explain. It's just that I've known Jerry for many years. I suppose he's like . . . like family."

He stood before her with his feet apart, his fists doubled at his sides. He was dressed in faded jeans and a black tank top. "Good for him. Maybe you'll give up piano for this Jerry Grosbeck."

She gasped. "Never! Oh, never!" She shook her head and her brown curls bounced.

Kyle turned to go and Elizabeth touched his arm and he stopped and looked down at her, his dark blond brow lifted in question, his eyes watchful.

"I'm sorry that I didn't tell you about Jerry before someone else did." She knew it must have been Aster, but she didn't accuse her. "I didn't think it would matter."

"Of course not," Kyle said coldly.

Elizabeth bit the inside of her bottom lip. "I have to go now. I'll see you later and we can talk more after practice."

"I have a date tonight."

Her heart stopped, then thudded on. "You do?" It hurt more than she thought possible.

"With Aster."

He looked cruelly pleased with himself. She lifted her chin high and forced a smile. "Then I'll see you tomorrow."

He shrugged. "Maybe."

Her legs wobbled and she wondered if they'd support her to the cabin. She watched Kyle stride away; then she turned and stumbled toward the cabin.

SIX
Aster

Elizabeth leaned against the closed cabin door, her chest rising and falling. Her music books tumbled to the floor and she jabbed her finger toward Aster. "You! You read my letter from Jerry! You told Kyle about Jerry!"

Aster slowly pushed herself off her cot and tugged her suntop down to meet her white shorts. "I did?"

Belinda scrambled off her cot and dashed to Elizabeth's side. "What happened? Your face is red and you're crying!"

Elizabeth pushed past Belinda and stood face to face with Aster. "Why are you doing this to me? What have I done to you?"

Jenny gasped and Belinda grabbed for Elizabeth's arm.

"I'm not going to hit her," said Elizabeth coldly. She wanted to be young again when she had had the freedom to punch anyone who got in her way. She leaned down so that her nose almost touched Aster's. "How could you hurt Kyle so much?"

Aster cleared her throat and stepped back, then plopped down on her cot. "Get away from me, Elizabeth

Johnson! You'll be very sorry if you do anything to hurt me!"

Elizabeth doubled her fists, fighting against the strong urge to leap on Aster. "I want you to stay away from my mail. I want you to stay away from me! And if you think this little trick of yours will break up Kyle and me, you're wrong!" But hadn't it worked already? "Kyle and I will work this out. Your little date tonight with him doesn't mean anything!" She stepped forward and Aster cringed back, her face white, her blue eyes wide with fear. "And once he learns how you got your information about Jerry, he won't have anything more to do with you."

"I haven't said that I told him in the first place. You don't know if I did or not. It might have been anyone who would bother to find out a little more about you."

"No one else would care to." Elizabeth stopped. Ned might. But that would mean that he'd have to get into the cabin when no one else was around, then look through her things until he found the letters from home.

Abruptly Elizabeth turned away. She heard Jenny sniffling as she picked up her books. Belinda stood at Elizabeth's cot, her face white, her eyes filled with concern.

"I'm all right," Elizabeth said in a low voice that caught in her throat. Would she really be all right until she could settle this with Kyle? Would he even let her settle it with him? He had been so angry, so hurt.

Slowly Elizabeth sank to her cot and stared across the cabin. The note lay in a crumpled ball near the door. She shot up, but before she could leap toward the note, Jenny grabbed it.

"Is that for me to see, Jenny?" said Aster with a wicked chuckle.

"It's mine!" cried Elizabeth as she reached for Jenny.

Jenny shivered, then pushed the wad into Elizabeth's trembling hand. "It must be yours." Jenny's voice cracked and she ducked her head and walked back to her cot.

Elizabeth gripped the paper and the sharp edges pressed into her palm. She caught her bottom lip between her teeth and fought against the overwhelming anger that surged through her, anger toward whomever had talked to Kyle and anger that someone was going to try to make trouble for her because of her terrible past.

Belinda touched Elizabeth's jean-clad knee and Elizabeth looked up. Belinda shook her head. "I'm sorry I have to leave you right now when you need a friend, but I have class in a few minutes. Will you be all right?"

Elizabeth nodded and her eyes filled with tears at the gentleness in Belinda's tone.

As the door closed behind Belinda, Aster jumped up. "I'm getting out of here. Come on, Jenny."

Jenny shook her head slowly. "I'm staying."

Aster's eyes widened. "What? I want you with me. I want to talk to you."

Jenny shook her head. Her hands trembled as she clutched her pillow against her chest. "I'll meet you later, Aster. I have some things to do first."

Aster slammed out of the cabin and Elizabeth muttered, "Good riddance."

In the silence that followed, Elizabeth could hear Jenny's breathing and the crackle of the note in her hand. She forced the anger to drain from her; then she slowly rubbed the note out flat. If Kevin was here right now, he'd find a way to trace the paper and the printing. He felt he was already a great detective even though he was only fourteen years old. But Kevin was home on the Johnson farm now and not here in Pine Valley Music Camp.

"Elizabeth?"

She looked over at Jenny. She was sitting on the edge of her cot, her hands locked tightly in her lap, her face as white as her pillowcase. "Yes?"

"I . . . I wrote that."

Elizabeth gasped. "What?"

"That note. I wrote it."

"Why?"

Jenny burst into tears and covered her pale face with trembling hands. Her shoulders shook and the rough sobs filled the room.

Elizabeth hesitated, then walked to Jenny and sat beside her, slipping a long arm around her. "I want to help you, Jenny."

Jenny stiffened, then shook her head and the tears flowed harder and faster.

Elizabeth slowly drew Jenny closer and patted her back and spoke soothing words to her the way her mom did when Elizabeth was upset.

Finally Jenny lifted her head. Her nose and eyes were red and her face wet. She sniffed hard as she reached for a tissue in a small pack beside her cot. She wiped away her tears, then balled the tissue and held it tightly. "Elizabeth, I like you. I think you're nice, sometimes too nice to Aster. But I know why you're nice."

Elizabeth cocked her brow. "You do?"

Jenny nodded, then pushed a stray strand of blonde hair out of her face and hooked it over her ear. "I know that you're a Christian."

"I am."

Jenny looked down at the floor, then at Elizabeth. "I

am, too, but I don't act like one and I haven't told anyone because I felt embarrassed about it." Fresh tears filled her eyes. "I'm so ashamed!"

Elizabeth patted Jenny's clenched hand. "I'm sorry, Jenny."

Jenny dabbed away her tears. "I wrote that note to warn you that someone—Aster—had found out that you're an aid kid. She's going to use that against you somehow."

"But I'm not an aid kid."

"You're not? But Aster read it right in that letter from Jerry."

"She did find it and read it!"

Jenny hung her head and her blonde hair slipped forward to block her face. "Yes. I told her not to, but she never listens to me."

"But I really am not an aid kid."

Jenny lifted her head and tucked her hair behind her ears. "You're not?"

"No. Once I was, but I was adopted by the Johnson family when I was thirteen."

"Then Aster can't hurt you!"

Elizabeth sighed. "Only my pride, but I will handle it somehow. I might be able to stop her before she really gets started."

"How?" Jenny twisted around on the cot, her knee bent, so she could look at Elizabeth.

"Today we have to tell a little about our backgrounds. If I tell that I am adopted, then Aster won't have anything to use." A shiver ran down Elizabeth's back. Would she be able to tell that to the other students without falling apart?

A smile spread across Jenny's face. "That will surprise Aster."

Elizabeth laughed softly. "Good."

Later in the classroom Elizabeth's breath caught in her throat as she realized it was her time to tell a little about herself. Slowly she stood beside her seat and silently asked the Lord to help her once again. She caught Jenny's eye and smiled. Jenny smiled back as she locked her hands together in her lap.

Elizabeth took a deep breath. "My name is Elizabeth Johnson. I've always wanted to play the piano. But when I was young, I couldn't. I was an aid kid." She paused and heard the gasp from Aster that she'd waited for. She smiled and lifted her head high. "Then the Johnsons took me to live with them and adopted me. Vera Johnson—my mom—started teaching me piano; then Rachael Avery accepted me as a student and I've been taking lessons from her ever since. I've had several recitals and played in three competitions and won two of them. I came here to further my career and to have a chance to practice more without the interruptions that come from having a family around all the time." Elizabeth sat down and butterflies fluttered in her stomach. She glanced toward Aster who was sitting with her head bent, her face red. Elizabeth grinned behind her hand, then listened to the next person.

After class Elizabeth walked slowly outdoors and Belinda ran up to her and grabbed her arm.

"I didn't know that you were adopted. How romantic! And to be taking lessons from the famous Rachael Avery! Oh, Elizabeth! I envy you so much! You have everything, don't you? A wonderful family, good looks, an absolutely fantastic piano teacher, and even a boyfriend."

Elizabeth smiled. She didn't know what to say. Before

she could think of anything, several students who had never spoken to her before spoke and smiled. The aroma of fried chicken for supper filled the air.

With a spring to her steps Elizabeth walked toward the dining hall. Suddenly someone gripped her arm and jerked her around. Aster stood there, glaring in anger. Elizabeth laughed aloud and Aster's face flamed.

"You really think you're great, don't you, Elizabeth Johnson? Well, you aren't! You might have all these people cheering for you, but Kyle Grey won't and never will."

Elizabeth pried Aster's fingers loose and brushed off her arm. "I will see about that, Aster. I'll talk to Kyle. We're friends, good friends. He won't stay angry with me." But would he?

"You won't have a chance to talk to Kyle." Aster shook her head. "I'll keep him so busy that he won't have time for you." Her blue eyes narrowed. "The only reason he hangs around you is because you remind him of his sister Beth. That's the only reason!"

Elizabeth gasped. Was it true? He had called her Beth several times. Beth had played the piano, and she played the piano, too.

Aster laughed, then sailed away in triumph.

"Don't listen to her," whispered Belinda.

Elizabeth looked toward the woods where she and Kyle had walked. An icy band tightened around her heart. Maybe Kyle didn't care about her at all. Maybe he never had, and never would.

"Let's go eat dinner, Elizabeth," said Belinda.

"You go ahead. I'm not hungry." Elizabeth turned toward the path that led to her cabin.

SEVEN
The audition

Elizabeth rubbed her damp palms on a tissue, stuffed it in her purse, then crossed her long legs and rubbed her soft burgundy skirt over her knees. Megan Tol's piano audition was coming to an end. Elizabeth looked around the near empty room in desperation. She was next and Kyle hadn't come to wish her the best. But then she should have known he wouldn't come. He hadn't spoken to her since she'd seen him outside her cabin and he'd told her that he knew about Jerry. Aster had certainly been hard at work to keep Kyle away from her.

Megan hit a wrong note and Elizabeth cringed. Oh, it would be terrible to miss a note with Mr. Brazer and Mr. Clearmont sitting right in the middle of the second row so they could see the player as well as hear him.

What was Mr. Brazer thinking right now? Was he just waiting for her to audition so that he could tell her that she hadn't made it, that she'd never make it as a concert pianist? Elizabeth frowned. She didn't dare think like that or she'd be too nervous when she played.

The floor creaked beside her and she turned her

head. Her heart leaped as Kyle sat down beside her, his long legs almost touching the chair ahead.

"Hi," she whispered with a smile. She wanted to lean against him and tell him that she'd missed him and that she was sorry that she hadn't told him about Jerry.

Kyle laid his arm across the back of her chair and leaned his head close to hers, his mouth almost touching her ear. She shivered as a thrill ran through her. She could smell his cologne.

"I hope that you get the part, Elizabeth. I want you to. You're a great pianist."

She turned her head slightly. "Thanks. I'm so glad you came."

His warm lips touched her cheek in a kiss and her heart beat so loud that she was sure he could hear it even over Megan's finale. She almost turned her head so that their lips would meet, but she sat very still and Kyle stood and walked quietly away.

Megan stood near the baby grand and bowed, then walked away. The door opened and closed behind her and Elizabeth stood up, took a deep breath, and walked to the front. She sat at the piano, smiled at the two men just as Rachael Avery had taught her to do, then touched the ivory keys. She would play as she'd never played before! Her cheeks glowed with the remembrance of Kyle's kiss and softly spoken words.

She struck the first chords, then played with the music flowing from her and through her. When she finished she sat with her head bowed, her hands resting on the bench on either side. Finally she slipped off the bench, smiled at the judges, and walked off with her head held high and her skirt swirling around her knees.

She stepped into the bright sunlight and sighed with

relief. Her audition was over and she'd done well, very well, in fact. She looked around for Kyle, but the only person she saw was Barney Little carrying his flute and music.

Tomorrow she'd learn the outcome of the audition. Tomorrow she'd know if she or Ned or maybe even one of the other piano students had been chosen. Ned had already auditioned and there were two others to go.

Slowly Elizabeth walked toward the fountain. The rest of the day was free time for her and she thought of the letters she could get written. She glanced toward the pool area. Maybe she should walk over and see if Kyle was there. A few days ago she'd have known his schedule, but not now, not since Aster.

Elizabeth frowned. What poison was Aster trying to spread today? An ant crawled across Elizabeth's toes and she lifted her foot and brushed it off. She rubbed the side of her white sandal with the high heel of her other shoe. It was hard to walk on the ground in these shoes, but it was worth it to look her best for the audition.

With a sigh Elizabeth walked toward her cabin. She'd better change before she did anything else. Jeans and tennis shoes or sandals with low heels were the only things comfortable enough to wear around camp.

Would she be chosen for the solo piano part?

Her stomach cramped and she stopped in the middle of the path. She just couldn't think about it now or she'd be a nervous wreck by tomorrow.

A squirrel chattered noisily and birds sang and flew. Small animals scurried in the underbrush. The scent of pine hung heavy in the air.

Slowly Elizabeth walked along the path. Kyle had kissed her. Kissed her! What did it mean? Was it a friend kissing a friend, or was it more? Gingerly she touched her cheek, then quickly pulled her hand away. She wasn't Susan who fell for every boy who walked across her path!

She opened the cabin door and Belinda jumped, her face flushed, then she laughed self-consciously. Belinda was wearing a sundress with multicolored flowers all over it. Her auburn hair was brushed to a shine and clipped back with two tiny gold barrettes.

"Hi," said Elizabeth, kicking off her shoes.

"You got a letter," said Belinda.

Elizabeth looked on her cot and on the stand beside her cot. "Where is it?"

Belinda giggled nervously as she opened her purse. "I didn't read it. Honest! I picked it up at the office when I saw it was for you and I put it in my purse for safekeeping because I knew you'd be gone for a while." She held the white envelope out to Elizabeth. "It's from Jerry."

Elizabeth hesitated, then grabbed the envelope and ripped it open. He knew today was her audition and he probably wanted to wish her the best.

"I have to go," said Belinda. "I'm meeting Barney so we can practice together." She flushed, then giggled. "I really mean practice."

Elizabeth nodded with a smile. "I believe you."

"If I was gorgeous, you wouldn't believe me so fast," snapped Belinda.

Elizabeth blinked in surprise. "What's wrong, Belinda?"

Belinda shook her head, her mouth drooping.

"I think you're very attractive, Belinda. And I'll bet Barney does, too."

"Then why hasn't he kissed me? Just once I'd like to have him kiss me or hold my hand!"

"Maybe he's shy."

Belinda rolled her eyes. "Not Barney. He just thinks I'm a good old buddy or something. He doesn't know that I'm a girl with feelings."

"I'm sorry, Belinda."

"Yeah, me, too." Belinda walked out and closed the door with a snap; then all was quiet in the cabin except for Belinda's alarm clock. The ticking seemed louder than usual.

Elizabeth sighed, then slowly changed into jeans and a gold tee shirt. She buckled sandals on her bare feet, then sat on her cot cross-legged and tried to think of something she could have said to Belinda to cheer her up.

Finally Elizabeth shrugged and reached for Jerry's letter. Right now she'd have to think of the man in her life instead of Belinda's.

Elizabeth unfolded the lined paper and rubbed her fingers across it. Just a few days ago this had been in Jerry's hands; now it was in hers. She smiled.

Dear Elizabeth,
What's this about a guy named Kyle Grey?

Elizabeth gasped and stared down at the words. Had she read right? But how had Jerry heard about Kyle? She rubbed her eyes, then continued to read.

I hear that you met the lifeguard and are spending a lot of time with him. I thought you loved me. I hope you don't come home and tell me that you never want to see me again.

Yesterday I got a letter from someone at your camp. It looked like a girl's writing. Anyway, she said that she knew that I was here waiting for you while you were there

playing around with this Kyle Grey. Is that true? I won't
believe anything until I hear it from you.
   Don't you love me anymore?

   Elizabeth stopped reading and looked into space. She
still loved Jerry but she loved Kyle, too. She gasped and
clapped her hand over her mouth.
   She loved Kyle!
   She shook her head. Maybe it was love as a sister
would love a brother. She chewed her bottom lip. How
could she love both Jerry and Kyle? It just wasn't
possible, was it?
   She squirmed uncomfortably. There were different
kinds of love. She loved both of them differently. And
she didn't want to hurt either of them. But right now
she felt as if she loved Kyle more than she loved Jerry.
Maybe it was because Kyle was here and Jerry was a
long way away.
   She rubbed her hand across her eyes, then finished
the letter.

   Elizabeth, I am glad that you went to music camp
because I know that's what you wanted. I want you to
make it as a concert pianist because that's what you want.
Just don't forget me as you go along. If it's true about this
Kyle Grey guy, then tell me where I stand with you. I'll be
waiting for your answer. I'm glad you'll be home soon. I
miss you a lot.

   Elizabeth dropped the letter on the cot and shook her
head. What a mixed-up life!
   She narrowed her eyes as she looked toward Aster's
part of the room. It had to be Aster who'd written to

Jerry. Who else would want to? Well, what did it matter now? It was done and it couldn't be undone.

Impatiently Elizabeth jumped up and crammed the letter in her purse. This was one letter that Aster would not get a chance to read!

She pulled out her stationery and picked up a fine-tip ballpoint pen. She'd write to Jerry and take it to the office so that it would go out in tomorrow's mail. Jerry deserved to hear from her immediately and he deserved to hear the truth even if it hurt him. She did love Kyle.

She held the paper and stared dreamily across the room. She loved Kyle and he'd kissed her. If she'd turned her head, his lips would have met hers. She sighed and touched her mouth with the tips of her fingers. Oh, what was she doing?

She looked at the blank paper, then slowly told Jerry how she'd met Kyle and about seeing the bears and how Kyle helped her practice and took long walks with her and talked about her future as a concert pianist. She didn't tell Jerry about the kiss on the cheek. She ended the letter with:

Jerry, I don't want to hurt you. I do love you. We've been through a lot together and I'll never stop loving you. But right now I love Kyle, too. Sometimes he's so sad because of his sister Beth. She died this past winter and he still misses her a lot. I want to take away some of his sorrow if I can.

I told you that I didn't want us to date just each other. You go with other girls and I'll go with other guys and then someday when we're old enough and we still love each other, we'll talk about a different arrangement.

I'm sorry. Don't be hurt. I'll always love you.

She sighed as she signed her name, folded the letter and pushed it into the envelope. She licked it shut, stamped it. In two or three days Jerry would read this. She held it to her and almost decided not to send it.

"I must!" she whispered with a sharp shake of her head.

Just then the door opened and Aster stepped inside, then hesitated when she saw Elizabeth.

"You don't have to run away, Aster." Elizabeth walked toward her and Aster's face turned a sickly gray. "I know that you wrote to Jerry, but I wrote back to him and told him what I felt I had to. I could use a lot of energy being angry at you, but it wouldn't do any good. You want to make trouble for me for some strange reason, so do what you must, but it won't do any good." Elizabeth tapped Aster's bare arm. "You can't hurt me. You can't even come close to hurting me."

Aster clamped her mouth closed tightly and narrowed her eyes to slits. "I wish you had never come here! I hate you!"

"I'm sorry about that. But that's your problem, not mine."

"I can't understand you. Not at all!"

Elizabeth shrugged and walked out of the cabin, her head high. Once she would have had to get even with Aster, fight with her, hate her back, but now it wasn't necessary. Elizabeth smiled. Maybe she was growing up at last, growing more like Jesus every day.

EIGHT
Lost in the woods

Elizabeth nervously fingered the silver chain around
her neck as she sat in the classroom, waiting for the
audition announcements. She glanced around quickly.
Where was Kyle? Last night she'd seen him briefly and
he'd said that he would meet her this morning to sit
with her for the news. Oh, but she needed him right
now! Had he overslept? Maybe he was walking through
the woods from his house right this minute.

She crossed her legs and her jeans felt almost too
tight and her blouse too hot. Why didn't the hands on
the clock move faster? She couldn't wait a minute
longer to hear the outcome.

A movement at her side startled her. She turned her
head, expecting to see Kyle, but Ned Everett stood
there, then slowly sank down in the seat next to her.

"I don't think I can handle much more of this
waiting," he said in a low voice as he sat with his short
legs stretched out and crossed at the ankles and his
arms folded across his stocky chest. He was wearing
brown dress slacks and a short-sleeved tan shirt opened

at the throat. He looked over at Elizabeth. "Aren't you nervous at all?"

"Am I!" She blew out her breath. "I've been trying to calm down. I can't wait to hear who was chosen."

Ned abruptly sat up straight and twisted around toward her. "Are you kidding?"

She frowned. "What do you mean?"

"I heard you play, Elizabeth." Ned jabbed his fingers through his light brown hair. "You were great, brilliant, and any other word to describe excellent."

"What about you? You were so sure you'd get it."

"I know." He shook his head. "I made a poor start and had to start over. I was really mad at myself! And then I came in when you auditioned and you didn't miss a note and the mood was right and everything. I really think you'll get it."

Her heart leaped and she squeezed her hands together. "Do you really think so? Oh, I want it! But I know you do, too. I'll really be sorry if you don't get it." She grinned. "But I'll be even sorrier if I don't."

He grinned and nodded. "Yeah, that's how I feel." He hit his fist into his palm. "Oh, but I wanted this! Why did I mess up?"

She patted his arm and smiled. "Maybe it wasn't as bad as you thought. We always think our mistakes are worse than they are."

He raised his brows. "Oh, sure."

"Well, we'll soon know, won't we?" She looked around the crowded classroom. Most of them already knew if they were going to play in the symphony. Most of the instruments had been announced yesterday.

"There's Mr. Brazer," whispered Ned tensely.

"Oh!" Elizabeth looked around frantically for Kyle.

She needed him with her right now! She saw Barney and Belinda sitting together and she knew both of them were to play their flutes in the symphony, but first chair was still to be announced.

A few minutes later when Belinda was chosen first-chair flute Elizabeth clapped louder than anyone. She knew Belinda could barely sit still in her excitement and happiness.

"I can't stand the suspense," whispered Ned close to her ear and she agreed completely.

She heard Jenny called for second-chair oboe and Aster first-chair violin, but she was too tense to clap. She locked her fingers together in her lap and pushed her feet tight against the floor. Her feet felt sweaty inside her tennis shoes and she wished that she'd worn her sandals, but she had planned on taking a walk with Kyle afterward and she hadn't wanted to take time to run back to the cabin to change.

Ned gripped her hand. "Here it comes, Elizabeth," he whispered hoarsely.

Elizabeth's back ached from sitting so rigidly. She held her breath for a moment, then slowly released it.

"Piano students," said Mr. Brazer as he looked over the class. "You all know that only one person can be chosen for the symphony. The rest of you will still have an opportunity to play before the school at the free-style program the last day of camp." He cleared his throat. "Mr. Clearmont and I have chosen for piano this year . . . Ned Everett."

Ned collapsed back against his seat, his eyes wide in surprise. Elizabeth gasped, then from deep inside she felt scalding tears rise. She had to get out before she cried in front of everyone. Her heart thudded so loud she was sure everyone could hear it over what Mr. Brazer was saying about practice time.

Frantically Elizabeth scrambled past Ned, then rushed to the door and out. She gulped great gulps of the cool morning air and tried to stop trembling. She should have been chosen! Even Ned had said she played better. Why hadn't she been picked instead of Ned?

Giant tears filled her eyes and rolled down her pale cheeks. Where was Kyle when she needed him so badly?

She looked toward the woods, but he wasn't in sight. She had to find him. She had to tell him her disappointment and cry on his broad shoulder.

With a strangled sob she ran to the woods on the path that he said led through the woods to his house. A twig caught at her hair and she yelled in pain as a few strands of hair were pulled out.

"Kyle," she whispered urgently between sobs. "Where are you?"

Desperately she ran around two large oaks and her foot caught on an exposed root and she sprawled to the ground, the breath knocked out of her. She lay there, sobbing into the dead leaves and musty soil. She had been so sure she was going to win, especially after what Ned had said. How could she survive now?

Weakly she pushed herself up and brushed dirt from her face and pulled leaves from her curls. Birds called overhead. Animals scurried in the underbrush and squirrels chattered noisily. But there was no sign or sound of Kyle.

Elizabeth blinked tears away and looked helplessly around. Where was the path she'd been following? Had she been so blinded by tears that she'd missed the path?

She sniffed and swallowed hard and pressed her hand on her heaving chest. She had to find the path and find Kyle.

Her face glowed with heat as she slowly walked around, her head down, her eyes bright with unshed tears. She couldn't see the path at all. She lifted her head and looked all around, turning slowly. A twig snapped under her foot and she jumped. The trees grew too close together to see very far. Nothing looked familiar. Once Kyle had showed her a deer trail, but even that wasn't in sight.

Was she lost?

She gasped, her eyes wide in alarm. Was she lost? Just how large were these woods? Maybe she'd walk around for days and never find her way out or find Kyle. She shivered and wrapped her long arms around herself. She swallowed hard, then called, "Kyle!" Then louder. "Kyle! Kyle, can you hear me? Kyle, it's me, Elizabeth!"

She waited and only silence met her ears. Nothing moved. No birds sang and she realized she'd frightened them all away as well as any ground squirrels or chipmunks.

She covered her face and sobbed. "Please, heavenly Father, send Kyle to get me out of here!"

Slowly she walked around trees, ducking low branches and sidestepping brambles and wild raspberry bushes that tugged at her jeans and snagged her blouse. She stared down at a long, red scratch on her arm, then whimpered softly.

She remembered years ago when she'd first moved to the Johnson farm, when she was still Libby Dobbs, aid kid. She'd gotten lost in the woods near their farm buildings. She had thought she'd be lost forever but Ben had found her.

"Kyle will find me," she whispered with a sob. "He will!"

Fear pricked her skin as she walked. Which way was camp? Which way was Kyle's home? Her stomach knotted painfully. She frowned as she stopped near a tall pine. She was a big girl now, no longer a scared little aid kid. She would not panic!

Just then she heard a great crashing noise deeper in the woods. Her head shot up and her eyes widened as she clutched the front of her blouse with a trembling hand. Was it Kyle coming for her, running to find her and save her?

"Kyle!" She plunged through the woods in the direction of the sound. "Kyle! You found me!"

She rounded a large hickory nut tree, then stopped dead, her eyes wide, her mouth gaping in terror. She gulped and clutched at her throat. Just two feet in front of her stood a black bear with two cubs beside it.

The bear's eyes were like small marbles in its big head. Its nose looked a little like a pig's snout. Burrs were caught in its fur. It opened its mouth and growled, then dropped on all fours and Elizabeth screamed in terror at the top of her lungs. Finally she forced her legs to move and she sped away, her heart racing wildly, perspiration running down her face and body. She screamed again, then again.

Was the bear chasing her? Just how fast could a bear run?

Frantically she looked over her shoulder and as she did her toe caught on a root and she plunged to the ground. Any minute now the bear would be on her and

tear her into little pieces. She sobbed and pushed herself up. How could she run another step?

She looked around and the bear was running toward her, swaying sideways as it ran. Elizabeth yelped and ran. Should she climb a tree? Did bears climb? Why hadn't she learned about bears in school so that she'd know what to do at a time like this?

She giggled hysterically. Who would have thought there would ever be a time like this?

A branch slapped her face and she cried out in pain but kept running. Pain stabbed at her side and she yearned to fall to the ground and just lie quietly and catch her breath and cool off. Carefully she glanced over her shoulder. The bear wasn't in sight. She stopped and looked and listened. Had the bear given up?

Elizabeth's chest heaved as she gasped for breath. She slowly sank to the base of a large oak and sat huddled against the rough bark, her knees touching her quivering chin. The pain eased from her side. She gulped great gasps of air that seemed to burn her dry throat.

"Kyle," she whimpered again, then shouted, "Kyle!" She pressed her head back against the tree trunk and fought against the tears that threatened to flow. "Kyle! Come get me! It's me, Elizabeth!"

Finally the rubbery feeling left her legs and her breathing became normal. She dabbed the perspiration off her forehead and tugged a twig from her curls.

A bee buzzed around her and she dodged and it flew away. Silence and heat pressed in on her and she wanted to scream and scream and never stop. Where were the trucks and cars and honking horns? Where were shouting and laughing people and instruments tuning up for a concert? Where was Kyle?

Elizabeth pushed herself up and stood with her feet apart, her hands resting on her waist. Butterflies fluttered in her stomach and shivers ran up and down her spine.

"Kyle!" she shouted again, then again until her throat ached. Why didn't he hear her? Why didn't anyone hear and come for her? Was she destined to stay lost in the woods forever?

Tears welled up in her hazel eyes and slowly spilled to run down her flushed cheeks. She knuckled them away only to have more follow.

Just then she heard a rustling noise and twigs snapping. The bear was coming after her again!

In panic she rushed ahead, away from the sounds. She wouldn't stay to be a bear's meal! She was Elizabeth Gail Johnson, concert pianist, not food for a black bear.

NINE
News about Kyle

Elizabeth leaped over a small stream, landed crookedly on her foot, and fell heavily to the moss-covered ground. She tried to push herself up, but her strength was gone. She sobbed against her arm. This was the end and she didn't have the strength to do anything about it. The bear had her for sure.

Something warm touched her face and she screamed and closed her eyes tighter, pulling into herself.

"Elizabeth, you're safe." Strong arms gathered her close and she opened her eyes to see Kyle's dear face almost touching hers.

"Kyle!" She flung her arms around him and pressed her face into his neck and sobbed.

He cradled her in his strong arms, his face buried in her curly hair. "I heard you call me, but I couldn't find you. I saw the bears and I was afraid."

Finally the tears stopped and she lifted her head and touched his face. "It's you. It's really you and I'm not dreaming. I asked God to send you to find me and he did. Oh, I'm glad to see you!"

"Why are you here, Elizabeth? I thought we agreed to meet in the classroom so you could hear the outcome of the auditions."

She shivered and her face puckered up. "Oh, Kyle!"

"What is it?"

"I waited for you and you didn't come."

"I was coming." He touched her cheek. "I couldn't miss that even if I was still mad."

"Don't be mad, Kyle. I don't want you to be. I'm sorry that I didn't tell you about Jerry. Aster shouldn't have, but she did. I was angry, but I got over that." Elizabeth looked down at Kyle's strong arm around her, then up into his dear face. "Jerry and I aren't really going together except once in a while. We're very close." She told him a little about Jerry and his background and how they'd first met, then how he'd come back into her life. "I didn't mean for this to hurt you, Kyle. You are special to me."

He smiled gently. "You're special to me. You have been since I first heard you play the piano."

She remembered that Aster had said Kyle only cared about her because she reminded him of Beth and she stiffened. "I . . . I think you'd better take me back. If I can walk." She grimaced as she moved. Every muscle ached and cried out for more rest, but she forced herself to stand.

"Why did you leave before class?"

She frowned. "I heard the announcement and I just couldn't stay there."

He glanced at his watch with a frown. "You told me to meet you at nine-thirty."

"Nine."

"Nine?" He shook his head. "But I was sure you said

nine-thirty. Then you know if you got it or not?"

"I didn't." She sniffed and wiped the back of her hand across her nose.

"You didn't?"

"Ned Everett did!" Her voice ended in a wail and she once again flung herself into Kyle's arms and pressed her face against his shoulder and sobbed.

"I am so sorry. You should have been chosen." He held her from him and she saw him through watery eyes. "I am sorry! It was Mr. Brazer again, wasn't it?"

"I think Mr. Brazer has something against me, Kyle. Ned said that I played better, yet Ned got it."

Kyle rubbed the tears off her face with his thumbs, then lightly kissed each cheek. "I'm going to have a long, serious talk with Mr. Brazer. Nothing will stop me this time."

"What good will it do to talk to him? He's already made up his mind."

"I don't care!" Kyle tugged on her hand and she walked with him. "I will at least get to tell him just what I think of him."

She stopped and he looked at her with his brows raised. "Kyle, you will only make trouble for yourself."

"I don't care."

She saw the stubborn set of his jaw and she knew nothing she could say would make any difference. "I'm so tired, Kyle. I just want to go back to the cabin and rest and get over feeling bad."

Kyle reached out and touched her cheek. There was a look of tenderness in his eyes, even though Elizabeth could tell he was still angry. He forced a brief smile. "Come on," he said. "I'll walk you back to your cabin. I have to go to work at the pool pretty soon anyway."

They walked the rest of the way down the path through the woods in silence. Elizabeth felt Kyle's tension, but she couldn't think of anything to say that would help.

When they reached the door of her cabin, Kyle turned to face her. She was shocked at the anger she saw in his face. "You can't stop me, Beth," he said, his jaw set. "Mr. Brazer isn't going to get away with this again. You are going to get to play in the symphony. It's your dream and you're going to do it!"

Elizabeth reached out and touched Kyle's arm. He looked so strange! "Kyle, why do you keep calling me 'Beth'?"

A quick look of fright crossed Kyle's face. "What?"

"You called me 'Beth.'"

"I did? Oh . . . well, I'm sorry. Just an old habit, I guess. I'll see you at the practice room tonight." Kyle suddenly looked very ill at ease. He turned quickly and strode toward the pool. As he did, a paper fluttered out of the folder he was carrying. He didn't see it fall, but Elizabeth did, and she picked it up.

"Kyle," she called. "You dropped something." As Kyle came back toward her, Elizabeth looked down at the paper she held in her hands. Her eyes widened in amazement. It was the first page of an original composition for violin and piano. The title at the top read "Springtime." And the composer was Kyle Grey! Elizabeth's trained eye could tell that the composition was good—*very* good! How she would love to play it! As Kyle reached her, she looked up at him, hardly knowing what to say. His face paled when he saw what she held.

"Kyle . . ." Elizabeth hesitated. She could tell that Kyle was upset by this. She asked the Lord to help her say the right thing. "You wrote this, didn't you?"

"Yes." Kyle looked as if he was in shock.

Suddenly, Elizabeth began to fit things together. Kyle's knowledge of classical music. His understanding of the way the music program at the camp operated. So many things he'd said since she met him. She looked up to meet his troubled gaze. "You play," she said simply. "You play the . . . violin."

Kyle nodded, unable to speak.

Why was Kyle so upset? Why had he hidden his musical ability from her? Elizabeth reached out and took Kyle's hand. "Kyle." His eyes met hers, full of pain. "Will you . . . bring your violin to the practice room tonight? Please?"

He looked at her for a long moment. "I'll think about it," he whispered, then turned quickly and hurried away.

All day long through classes and practice sessions, Elizabeth found her thoughts straying back to Kyle. Why did he keep calling her "Beth"? Why hadn't he told her about his ability to play the violin? Elizabeth knew that Kyle was really hurting inside, and she wanted to help him. He had helped her so much; now was her chance to do something for him. But what could she do?

TEN
"Spring time"

Elizabeth lifted her fingers from the keyboard as the last sounds of the Chopin Etude died away. She looked nervously toward the door of the practice room. Kyle had agreed to meet her here. He knew that her practice hour was from eight to nine, yet it was eight-ten and he wasn't here yet.

A tree limb tapped against the window, and Elizabeth jumped nervously. Her mind drifted back to the scene with Kyle that morning. Why had Kyle been so upset? What did his musical ability have to do with his sister, Beth? Elizabeth bowed her head and prayed quietly. "Father, help Kyle to have enough courage to come tonight. And help me to know how to help him."

Elizabeth sighed and opened her music. The Chopin B-flat Minor Sonata was difficult, and Mr. Brazer had been displeased with her progress at today's lesson. She was determined to get it perfect. She had just set her hands to the keys when she heard a quiet knock on the door. She got up from the piano bench and opened the door. It was Kyle. Elizabeth looked quickly and noticed that he had his violin case under his arm. He was also carrying the folder he had had with him that morning.

Elizabeth smiled and stepped back so that Kyle could come in. He stepped through the doorway without a word. When he came into the light, Elizabeth was alarmed to notice how pale Kyle was. He was breathing fast, and his hands were trembling as he set his violin case down on the chair.

She tried to think of something to ease the tension. Suddenly she smiled again. "Kyle," she asked, "would you help me with the phrasing in this Chopin piece? Mr. Brazer didn't like the way I did it today, especially here on the second score. I just can't get it right." Elizabeth sat down at the piano and began to play. "Do you think it should go like this—or like this?"

As she had hoped, Kyle seemed to relax a little. He sat down in the chair closest to the piano. "I think it's better the second way," he said. "But I think you want a little more *legato* on the last two measures. Then it flows more naturally into the next phrase."

Elizabeth tried it the way Kyle suggested. Something clicked and she knew that her problem with the piece was solved. "That's it, Kyle!" she cried. "Now listen to the whole thing and tell me what you really think—be honest!"

She turned to the music, closed her eyes for a moment, then opened them and began to play. As her fingers moved gracefully across the ivory keys, Elizabeth forgot that Kyle was sitting next to her. She forgot that she was worried about him. She forgot everything except the music. Elizabeth and the piano were no longer two separate things, but one unit, and

Elizabeth couldn't tell if the music was really coming from the piano—or from herself.

When the sonata was finished, she sat quietly for a moment, unable to move, to break the spell. Slowly she turned her head and smiled at Kyle. There was a little sparkle in his eyes, and a gentle smile on his lips. "You don't need for me to say anything," he said quietly. "You know how good you were. Your music isn't in the piano or in that score. It's in you, Elizabeth, and you just have to let it out. Just like. . . ." Kyle stopped suddenly and his face paled. He turned his face from Elizabeth and stared blankly out the small window.

Elizabeth reached over and took Kyle's hand. "Kyle," she said gently, "would you play for me? Please?" Silently she prayed for the Lord to help him.

Kyle turned to Elizabeth with a long, searching gaze. "You don't know what you're asking." His voice faltered. "I don't know if I can . . ."

"You can, Kyle," Elizabeth encouraged. "Please." Somehow she knew that it was very important that Kyle play for her tonight.

He looked at her again and she could see the pain in his eyes. Wordlessly he rose from his chair and went to his violin. Elizabeth quickly moved from the piano bench to the chair Kyle had just vacated and watched him prepare his instrument.

Kyle took out his bow first and carefully checked it. When he was satisfied, he applied a little rosin. Then he put down the bow and picked up the violin. It was a beautiful instrument, and Elizabeth could tell that it was very expensive. Kyle reached into his jeans pocket and pulled out a clean handkerchief and unfolded it and placed it against the left side of his neck. Carefully, he set the violin in place under his chin and began to tune it, first tightening and loosening the pegs while he gently plucked the strings, then trying the same thing with his bow.

Elizabeth watched Kyle carefully. She could tell that he was acting out a long-established habit. He had obviously played the violin for many years. But he was very upset. Kyle's hands were shaking and there was a thin film of perspiration on his upper lip. Elizabeth sat quietly, praying silently, waiting to see what would happen next.

When Kyle was satisfied that the violin was properly tuned, he placed it more firmly under his chin, set the fingers of his left hand along the strings, and raised the bow. Elizabeth heard him take a deep breath. Then he began to play.

It was a familiar warm-up exercise. At first Kyle's fingers seemed slow and a little clumsy, but Kyle forced them to work faster and faster. Elizabeth knew enough about violin technique to see that Kyle was very good, but he seemed out of practice.

There was a tiny light in Kyle's eyes and his mouth was beginning to lose its tenseness. When the exercise was over, he paused for a moment. He shifted his posture slightly and raised the bow again. Then Kyle began to play.

The first few notes were tentative, but the music quickly began to pick up strength and power. Elizabeth leaned back in her chair in amazement. She recognized the piece Kyle was playing. It was Bach's Unaccompanied Partita No. 3, one of the most difficult solo pieces in the violin repertoire!

Kyle's face had changed. There was a smoldering fire

in his eyes. He was no longer pale, but flushed with effort. And his tense posture had loosened so that his slim muscular body swayed slightly with the music. The music was so beautiful that Elizabeth could hardly bear it. She closed her eyes, and let it wash over her in waves. The music became more and more powerful as Kyle became more sure of himself, until with a final flourish, the piece ended.

Elizabeth's eyes remained closed for a moment, as she savored the incredible beauty she had just heard. Then she heard a sharp intake of breath from Kyle and opened her eyes. Kyle was crying, with tears streaming down his face. He clutched his violin to his chest, which was heaving with sobs.

Elizabeth rose from the chair and went to Kyle. She gently took the violin and bow from him and laid them carefully on a chair. Then she put her arms around him and held him close. When his sobs began to quiet a little, Elizabeth led Kyle to the piano bench and they sat down together, Kyle clinging tightly to Elizabeth's hand.

Kyle smiled at her weakly through his tears. "Sorry about that." He drew a long sigh. "I last played the 'Partita' at a joint recital with my sister, Beth. I haven't played since she . . . died. I didn't know if I could. I still don't know if I can. All my thoughts and goals in music were tied up with . . . her."

Elizabeth squeezed Kyle's hand. "If you can tell me, Kyle, I'd like to hear about Beth."

"What can I tell you about Beth? She was my twin sister and I loved her. We did a lot of things together. She studied piano and I studied the violin. From our very first lessons, we played together."

"You play beautifully, Kyle! You should be at Pine Valley as a student, not a lifeguard."

"I was last year. With Beth." Kyle's face clouded over and he was silent for a moment. "She wanted to play solo piano in the symphony. And she was the best student in the camp. But Mr. Brazer chose someone else. Beth was crushed. I wanted to punch Mr. Brazer, but she wouldn't let me. I wish I had! The boy he chose was good, but not as good as Beth. She played the way you do, Elizabeth."

She flushed with pleasure.

"Beth was uncertain of herself after that. She thought maybe she'd misjudged her own talent. But she was brilliant! I composed music just for us. We were going on tour together as soon as we could.

"And then. . . ." Kyle began to tremble. "Last winter we were ice-skating together on the lake. Beth was a terrific skater! She was trying to teach me some figures and skated away from me to show me what she wanted me to try." He drew a long shuddering breath. "She fell through the ice. I tried to get to her, I really did, but I couldn't. By the time they pulled her out, it was too late." Kyle looked up, staring at nothing. He was gripping Elizabeth's hand so hard it hurt. He closed his eyes, as though to blot out the picture he saw in his mind. "She shouldn't have died," he whispered after a long pause. "She had such great plans."

Elizabeth turned toward Kyle and took him in her arms. She felt his arms go around her and they sat for a moment without speaking. Then Kyle pulled away from her slightly, his eyes blank with despair. "I don't think I can play without Beth," he said. "All my dreams, my compositions, were for Beth. With Beth. Music reminds me that she's . . . gone."

Elizabeth put her hands on either side of Kyle's face. "Listen to me, Kyle. You have a God-given gift and you must share it with others. You'll never be happy unless you do."

"Is God special to you, Elizabeth?"

She nodded. "He is my heavenly Father and Jesus is my Lord and Savior."

"Beth talked about being born again. She told me about Jesus, but then she died."

"God loves you, Kyle. He wants to be a part of your life just as he was part of Beth's life and is part of my life, too. Each person has an emptiness inside him, a loneliness that no one can take away, that only God can fill."

"I know what you mean."

"God wants to help you every day of your life, Kyle. He wants to take away your sorrow and grief. He wants to fill your life with joy and love and peace."

Kyle nodded. "I saw the difference it made in Beth's life."

Elizabeth smiled and her heart leaped for joy. "Shall we pray together right now? We can talk to God and tell him how you feel." Elizabeth bowed her head next to Kyle's and quietly prayed. Then Kyle prayed. Tears filled Elizabeth's eyes and slowly ran down her cheeks. This was more exciting than winning a piano competition or even playing in the symphony.

Kyle looked up at her, his eyes filled with a new peace. "I've been so hungry to play again since I met you, Elizabeth. Each time I sat in the practice room with you, I wanted to get my violin and join in with you."

"I knew you knew a lot about music, but I never dreamed you played an instrument." She smiled up at him, then frowned slightly.

"What's wrong, Elizabeth?"

She studied her fingernails. "Kyle, you didn't spend time with me just because I reminded you of Beth, did you?"

He squeezed her shoulder. "No. And when I learned that you were in love with a guy back home, I was very upset."

Her heart stopped, then raced on. "You were?"

"I tried to tell myself that I was angry because you weren't really completely dedicated to the piano."

"And then?" She couldn't look at him. Her stomach tightened as she waited for his answer.

"I guess I was forced to realize that wasn't the *real* reason. I care a lot about you, Elizabeth. You're special to me."

"Kyle, Jerry isn't my boyfriend. I do love him, in a way. But we've known each other since we were kids, and we understand each other. But I care about you, too. I have since the first time we walked together."

Kyle stood up and pulled her to her feet. His arms went gently around her and he lowered his head until his lips met hers.

In a burst of happiness, Elizabeth put her arms around Kyle's neck and kissed him back. She never wanted the moment to end.

Kyle raised his head and looked at her for a moment. Their eyes met and there was no need for words. Suddenly, Elizabeth thought of something. "Kyle," she said hurriedly. "Did you bring your composition? The one I found this morning?"

"Yes, I did. It's right here."

"Kyle, could we play it. You and me?"

A shadow crossed Kyle's face for a moment. Then it was replaced with a smile. "Sure. I'd like that." Kyle got out the music, placed it on the piano, and then turned to get his violin. Elizabeth sat at the keyboard, and carefully read over the unfamiliar music. Kyle took his place behind her, settled his violin under his chin, and raised his bow. Elizabeth looked up at him and smiled.

"The tempo should go like this," Kyle said, beating out the rhythm with his bow. "I'll give the downbeat."

Elizabeth looked back at the piano and sat ready as Kyle softly counted out a measure. Then, in perfect accord, they began to play.

The piano score wasn't easy, and Elizabeth had to concentrate on the notes. She was hard pressed to keep up with the tempo Kyle had set. But what a beautiful piece it was! The piano and violin blended and complemented each other, playing melody, harmony, and counter-melody with a beauty that was musical poetry. It ended all too soon for Elizabeth.

She looked up at Kyle, her eyes shining. "Oh, Kyle!" she breathed. "It's lovely, just lovely. You must share it with others. You must!"

Kyle smiled down at her. "I think I can—now," he said. "My father knows an agent who will look at the piece. Maybe someday this will be played the way Mozart's early works are performed now."

Elizabeth glanced at her wristwatch. "Oh, oh, it's nine o'clock!" she exclaimed. "We've got to get going."

Kyle began to gather his music and put away his violin. "You know, I'd still like to talk to Mr. Brazer.

Don't worry, though," he grinned as he looked over his shoulder at Elizabeth. "I won't punch him now."

"I'd like to talk to him, too," Elizabeth said, thoughtfully. "I'd really like to find out why I wasn't chosen for the symphony. I can take the truth—I think!"

"Why don't we walk by his cabin and see if he's still up?" Kyle questioned.

"Good," Elizabeth said. "We'll go together."

ELEVEN
A decision

"Mr. Brazer, I would like to know why you chose Ned Everett over me when I performed much better than he did at the audition," said Elizabeth. Her voice was calm, but she gripped her hands together behind her back as she stood with Kyle in front of Mr. Brazer.

Mr. Brazer raised up on his toes, then settled down on his heels and stuffed his hands into his pants pockets. "I don't have to answer that question, Miss Johnson. My decision is made and it's final."

Elizabeth suddenly felt very closed in inside Mr. Brazer's small cabin. Mrs. Brazer had just gone out when they'd arrived. "I don't believe it was a fair decision, Mr. Brazer."

"I don't either," said Kyle sharply. "Last year's decision wasn't fair either and I've wanted to tell you ever since."

"And who did you think should have won last year?" asked Mr. Brazer with a scowl on his round face.

"Beth Grey, my sister."

"Then why isn't she here to speak for herself?"

"She's dead."

Mr. Brazer flushed and cleared his throat. "I didn't know."

"Did you feel that Beth was a good pianist?" asked Elizabeth.

Mr. Brazer cleared his throat again. "Of course she was good. But that doesn't mean she'd have made it as a concert pianist."

"She would have!" Kyle took a menacing step forward and Elizabeth caught his arm and tugged him back. "And she wanted desperately to play for the symphony last year. She would have, too, if someone else had been deciding."

Elizabeth gasped and Mr. Brazer puffed out his chest.

"Just what do you mean by that, young man?"

"I mean that you aren't fair. I don't know why, but I do think you already had decided ahead of time who was going to be chosen. You just went through the auditions because it was expected of you."

Elizabeth couldn't believe her ears, but on hearing what he said she decided that she agreed with him. "I think you're right, Kyle!" She looked at Mr. Brazer through narrowed eyes. "I think you picked Ned two weeks ago. I didn't have a chance. I'd like to know why."

Mr. Brazer's gray eyes darkened with anger. "You aren't a serious student, Elizabeth. In a few years you'll get married and forget about being a concert pianist. A man can get married, but he continues his career." He wagged his finger at Elizabeth. "Look at your piano teacher, Rachael Avery. She was on top but she let it go for a family. I say that a woman should find a different career, not one in this field."

Kyle doubled his fists. "I don't believe I'm hearing

this! How can you say such a thing? You have no right to judge!"

Elizabeth felt her anger rising and she fought against it. "Do you mean that if I'd been a boy, I would have been chosen this morning?"

"I didn't say that."

"But you do think that because I might not keep on with my career in music that I don't have the right to play in the symphony." Elizabeth's voice rose.

Kyle slipped his arm around her narrow waist. "Easy."

She clamped her mouth closed and glared at Mr. Brazer.

Mr. Brazer shrugged. "I believe it's time for you both to leave. It's after class time and I don't have to talk to you."

"I'll go see Mr. Clearmont," said Elizabeth, forcing back her anger. She would not say anything to Mr. Brazer that she'd regret later!

"That's what we should have done in the first place," said Kyle, turning with Elizabeth toward the door.

"Wait!" Mr. Brazer hurried around them to stand between them and the door. "I don't want any trouble. It's already too late to do anything about my decision."

"But you should have chosen Beth last year. Right?" asked Kyle grimly.

"I don't remember your sister."

Kyle growled deep in his throat and Elizabeth kept him from springing on the short man in front of them.

"But you do remember me," said Elizabeth very softly, very precisely. "If you weren't prejudiced, would I have been chosen?"

Mr. Brazer's face turned a brick red. "I am not prejudiced. I feel that a young man who is outstanding in piano deserves every break he can get."

"You answered my question. You said 'young man.' You wouldn't allow a girl to play." Elizabeth's eyes smarted with tears. It seemed so unfair! "We'll talk to Mr. Clearmont."

"No!" Mr. Brazer shook his gray head. "If it's that important to you, then yes, you did play the best. But Ned Everett is every bit as good. I wanted to give him every advantage."

"What about me?" cried Elizabeth, pointing to herself with a trembling finger. "It would have helped my career."

Mr. Brazer rubbed his hand over his balding gray head. "All right. You play the solo. I don't want the hassle."

"And what about Ned Everett?" asked Elizabeth coldly.

Mr. Brazer shrugged. "He won't play."

"But he'll be hurt!" Elizabeth shook her head in disbelief at the man's calloused behavior.

"It's in your hands now," said Mr. Brazer. "You tell him that I changed my mind."

Elizabeth looked helplessly up at Kyle. She really wanted the solo part, but she didn't want to have Ned hurt the way she had been this morning.

"I'll tell Ned," said Kyle.

Elizabeth shook her head. "No. He's excited about being chosen. I don't want to hurt him and I won't. We'll leave it the way it is, but I do plan to talk to Mr. Clearmont so this can't happen again."

Mr. Brazer jerked open the door and Elizabeth walked out with Kyle close behind. Tree toads sang along with peepers and bullfrogs. Music drifted from the practice rooms.

Kyle stopped Elizabeth near the fountain. "I want you to play in the symphony."

She shook her head, her hand on Kyle's arm. "Ned

was already chosen. It would break his heart if he had to step aside now. I can't do it to him. I'd feel rotten if I did."

Kyle sighed. "All right. I'll bet Beth would have made the same decision. But I wanted to hear you perform."

"I'll still be able to play the last day of camp for the free show." She gasped, then laughed. "Kyle, you and I will play together! We'll give the premier performance of your composition."

"We'll do it!" He grabbed her and danced around with her, laughing happily.

Elizabeth caught a glimpse of someone, then saw it was Aster. "I want to speak to Aster," Elizabeth said softly to Kyle.

"Not without me," said Kyle, keeping one arm around her waist. "Hello, Aster."

Aster's face blanched and she tossed her dark hair back. "Hello. I see you didn't listen to my little warning."

"About Jerry?" asked Elizabeth and Aster stepped back quickly. "Jerry and I have an understanding, Aster. He's not my boyfriend. I have every right to go with Kyle."

"Which I'm happy about," said Kyle. "After this, Aster, mind your own business."

Aster ran past them toward the cabin and Elizabeth leaned her head against Kyle, thankful that Aster couldn't make more trouble between them.

"Tomorrow we'll start practicing for the free show," said Kyle as he rubbed his cheek against Elizabeth's hair.

"It'll be the best music of the show!" She laughed excitedly, thinking of the show, and because she was close to Kyle and he was making her heart leap in a way that made her feel happy and confused at the same time.

On the day of the symphony Elizabeth sat with Kyle and listened as the music swelled around them. Ned was playing so well that tears filled her eyes. She smiled thankfully at Kyle as he squeezed her hand. If he hadn't taken her hand, she might have floated around the room. She saw a look pass between Belinda and Barney and she was glad that Barney had finally kissed Belinda. She'd been all bubbly and giggly last night and she'd whispered to Elizabeth that Barney had said he loved her.

After the last note Elizabeth clapped, then jumped to her feet and clapped harder. Soon everyone was standing and applauding. Ned stood beside the piano and bowed low. He looked as if he felt ten feet tall.

On the last day of camp Elizabeth slowly packed her bags, then looked around the cabin that had been her home for a month. She was glad to be going back to the Johnson farm to see her family, but she hated to leave her new friends. And Kyle.

She bit her bottom lip. Would Kyle really miss her, too? Tears stung her eyes and she picked up the last few things off her cot and stuck them into her bag. The last few days practicing together with Kyle had been heavenly. At five she'd board a bus for home and maybe never see Kyle Grey again.

She sniffed hard and dabbed her tears away with a tissue. She couldn't think sad thoughts now. In just a few minutes she and Kyle would be performing in front of the entire camp, and she had to be at her best for Kyle as well as herself. When she'd told Mr. Clearmont about the composition and about Kyle, he'd promised to have an agent in the audience that would contact Kyle later to talk about a tour.

Elizabeth shivered with excitement, then later as she stood backstage with Kyle she shivered again with nervous excitement. She looked up at Kyle and he seemed so calm and professional. Love for him washed over her and she leaned her head against his arm. He was dressed in a three-piece gray suit that complemented her apricot dress which fitted smoothly at her narrow waist and belled out to touch her toes.

"Are you all right, Elizabeth?" he whispered.

She lifted her head and smiled at him. "I love you, Kyle."

He smiled and kissed her softly. Her heart sounded like a drum in her ears as she waited for him to say that he loved her, too, but he turned back to listen to the instrumental trio onstage.

Just as they finished Kyle said, "They're quite good. Jenny's oboe made the group."

Elizabeth nodded, then smiled as Jenny walked offstage.

"I'm looking forward to hearing your music," said Jenny breathlessly. "I'm glad you're playing today, Elizabeth." She turned away, then looked back. "Thanks for your friendship. I appreciate it."

Elizabeth smiled and nodded. Jenny had finally been able to stand up to Aster and tell her that she was a human being with feelings and not a shadow or a slave. Aster had taken it very well and still wanted to be friends. Jenny had agreed.

Just then the announcer said, "This next number is composed by one of the local young men, Kyle Grey, who is an artist on the violin. On piano will be Elizabeth Johnson, a budding young concert pianist. They are going to play 'Springtime' for violin and piano. Please welcome them now. Elizabeth Johnson and Kyle Grey." He held out his arm toward them and they walked onstage hand in hand as the audience applauded.

Elizabeth bowed to the audience and Kyle nodded.

94

She sat at the piano and arranged her soft skirt as he picked up his violin.

She looked up at him and smiled and he smiled at her and her heart leaped with love.

He nodded slightly and she struck the first chord and he came in with the violin. The music began *forte* to show the pounding rain, then grew softer as the rain became gentler. The piano notes rolled as a steady stream of water and the violin picked up the sparkles and ripples. Flowers bloomed, new life began, children sang and played and danced.

Elizabeth's fingers flew over the keys and her entire being was involved with the music. She could hear the violin together with the piano and the music filled her so that she gave out more and more.

She touched the last note and silence filled the room. She looked up at Kyle and he smiled the most beautiful smile she'd ever seen in her life. He bowed toward her and the audience went wild and the applause almost deafened her.

Slowly she stood beside Kyle and curtsied while he bowed. He caught her hand and she curtsied again, this time to him. She peeked up at him and he bowed to her, then lifted her up.

"I love you," he said.

Her heart leaped and she squeezed his hand as the applause continued. "They want an encore," she said.

He nodded, then seated her at the piano. She watched as he picked up his violin and tucked it under his chin. He loved her! She laughed aloud, then played an encore with him for their wonderful audience.